Forever Determined

Forever Determined

*An inspiring novel of hope, courage,
and a woman's will to overcome adversity.*

CAROLINE ADAMS
KEITH MICHAEL PRESTON

ISBN: 9781796602258

Cover Art Designed by Thomas J. Zaffo

Typesetting & Layout by Monte Press Inc.

Printed in the U.S.A.

*In memory of our grandmother
whose journey inspired us to publish
this timeless story of hope and determination.*

We would like to extend a special thank you to our mother, Diane Preston, who constantly reminds us to follow our dreams.

We are forever grateful to our spouses, Terry Adams and Nancy Preston, and our father, George Preston, for their continued patience and support.

And lastly, we would like to show appreciation to the following individuals for their invaluable advice and ongoing help while creating this book: Barbara and Frank DeAngelo, Nicole Gilmore, Thomas Zaffo, and Veronica Reed.

THE EARLY YEARS
1926

CHAPTER 1

❧

Family Time

Pauline always dreamed of becoming a nurse. She lived in one of the poorest communities in Lodi, New Jersey, the tenement complex called Colonial Villa. It was a cluster of old, rundown apartment buildings that thousands of people called home. Water faucets leaked, paint peeled from the walls, and the radiators barely got hot during the cold winter months. Even though they lived in substandard conditions, most tenants didn't complain. They feared repercussions and couldn't afford to pay higher rents. It was 1926 and a time the country was experiencing tremendous economic growth and prosperity. However, the young families and retirees who filled these congested and poorly maintained neighborhood apartments weren't so lucky.

Colonial Villa was isolated from the main road and only tenants entered the close-knit community. The neighborhood was crammed with rows of thick brick structures, making it impossible to tell where one building started and another one ended, except for short walkways that created a pathway to each entrance.

Pauline lived with her parents and younger sister in the Rolfe building. Their second floor apartment was a dream location for families. It was situated at the end of a dead end street with a large patch of grass in front of the building where kids safely played until dusk. It was their private outdoor playground and a small perk for living in deplorable conditions. However, Pauline rarely went outside to play with the other children. She preferred to stay indoors and act as a pretend nurse with her younger sister, Josephine. Although they were just two years apart, the siblings looked and behaved very differently. In fact, strangers rarely believed they were related at all, never mind that they were sisters. At eight years old, Pauline's long, slender frame was a sharp contrast to her naturally wavy hair. Every night she attempted to tame her soft brown curls by combing her hair straight, ritualistically counting one hundred strokes before climbing into bed. Her full lips rarely parted into a smile or laugh, except when she played with Josephine. Pauline watched over and protected her younger sister, especially since they were polar opposites in every way. Full of life and energy, Josephine's plump figure balanced out her straight blond hair. Even with repeated teasing and back combing, her fine hair rarely stayed neatly tied up and fell loosely around her face. Upbeat and social, she yearned to play outdoors with the other kids but Josephine adored her older sister and stayed indoors when she wanted to play nurse.

It was a typical evening. Pauline and Josephine played together in the living room. Pauline's treasured book was by her side and Josephine's favorite doll rested on her lap. Ada, their mother, was busy preparing dinner for their father who wasn't home yet. Noticing the time, she entered the living room. "Come on girls, dad isn't going to be happy if you're still up. You haven't even changed into your night clothes yet." She tried to nudge the children up from the floor. Frail and depleted, the bruises around her eyes were finally starting to heal.

Josephine pleaded, "But mom, we just started playing together. Can we finish?" Pauline placed her hand on Josephine's chest and rested her ear to her other hand to listen through her imaginary stethoscope. A mouse ran across the room. They didn't flinch and continued playing.

Ada looked at her oldest daughter. She softened her eyes and said, "Maybe one day you could be a doctor or a nurse, Pauline. Would you like that?"

"I would love that!" Pauline said, flashing an uncharacteristic smile.

"Make sure you stay in school then. Okay, let's go girls. Your father will be home any minute and I don't want any trouble tonight."

Pauline nodded but didn't move. She pretended to listen to Josephine's heartbeat. "You're perfect…" Pauline's voice trailed off when she heard footsteps in the hallway.

Ada whispered, "Hurry up, he's home."

Hearing the creak of the front door open, the girls raced toward their bedroom. Harry stumbled down the hallway. His disheveled hair and red face after walking up two flights of stairs warned Ada that her husband had been out drinking again. She never knew what would set him off when he was in this state. She quickly grabbed the book and doll and shoved them under her apron, hoping he wouldn't notice. Stumbling further into the room, he saw what his wife had done. "How many times do I tell ya, they should be cleaning, not reading?"

"They need to get a good education. Pauline wants to be a nurse." She froze and cowered looking at the floor after noticing his face turning a deeper red.

"What did you say? They need to get a job, that's what they need."

Ada looked up. "Jobs? They're children. Besides, I want them to concentrate on their studying."

"Are you talking back to me again?" Harry reeled.

"No, but their education is the most important thing. Don't you want the best for them? They're your children after all."

Harry was furious that his wife was still talking. He stumbled toward her and put his face right up to hers. He said, "Who gives a damn? They're girls. Education means nothing for them."

From the bottom bunk bed, Josephine called out to her older sister, "Pauli, you awake?"

Pauline barely had time to answer when she heard her younger sister getting out of bed. "Josie, what are you doing? Get back in bed!" Pauline cried out as she climbed down the ladder and pushed her younger sister away from the closed door.

"I just want to see." Josephine moaned.

The two girls listened to the escalating voices of their parents. Now curious, Pauline slowly opened the door to peek out. Josephine crouched down below her sister.

Harry glanced at the table. "Where's my dinner? I expect it to be ready when I get home."

"I'm getting to it." Ada shuffled passed her husband.

Harry grabbed her arm. The sudden force caused Ada to stumble backward. She lost hold of her apron as the book and doll tumbled to the floor. Harry glanced down at the book while tightly clenching his fists. Looking up to meet his wife's gaze he yelled, "How many times do I tell ya, they're girls and shouldn't be studying. It's a waste of time. They'll be cooking and cleaning like you one day. That's what you should teach them."

"I want more for them. I don't want them to turn out like me."

"I'm tired of this nonsense. It's been going on too long now. I'm number one in this house."

"You're wrong. The girls are number one. They come first. That's how I look at it."

"Maybe I'm not getting through to you." Harry stepped closer to his wife.

"You can hit me all you want. I'll never change how I feel. They need to get out of this rotten place and life we have." Ada wasn't backing down.

"Rotten life?" Harry lunged toward her and the back of his hand struck her face. She shrieked from the blow. Seeing him raise his hand again, Ada stepped back and shielded her face. "You got some nerve talking to me like that." Harry swung at his wife again.

The girls gasped.

"One day I'm gonna take the girls and leave." Ada squared her shoulders and looked him straight in his eyes.

She went too far. Enraged, Harry violently swung and hit her again. She dropped to the floor.

"You don't deserve us. You never have." Ada slithered backward to further her distance from him.

Harry yanked off his belt and swung it at her. "Leave? You'll never take them away. You must have forgotten. I make the rules around here."

"But Pauline has dreams. I wanna make sure she fulfills them."

"Dreams? Now, I'm gonna make sure you keep your mouth shut." Harry unleashed another blow. Blood trickled over her eye.

Unafraid of her father's temper, Pauline raced in to try and help her mother. She jumped on his back. "Dad, stop it! Leave mom alone."

Ada screamed at her daughter, "Pauline, get out of here! Go back to your room with your sister."

Ada tucked her arms and legs together like a ball as Harry continued to swing the belt. With his free hand, he ripped Pauline off his back and tossed her against the wall. She tumbled to the floor as the peeling, chipped paint showered over her. Unable to move to protect her daughter from her husband's wrath, Ada screamed out to her, "Pauline, get back in your room and lock the door. Now!"

Harry was not done. With a fiery rage in his eyes, he looked at Pauline. "I'm tired of all of you. Today, you're all gonna get it."

Pauline's eyes widened as she sprinted passed him to the bedroom. She slammed the door shut, locked it, and pulled Josephine toward the bed. They both dropped to the floor, shimmying far under the bottom bunk bed. The two sisters were frightened and held onto each other. They had never seen him this angry before. They stayed under the bed and cried silently together as they listened to their mother's screams and the sound of a belt cracking from the other room.

At daybreak, sunlight glistened through the bedroom window. Pauline stirred and slowly opened her eyes. The silence was deafening. She nudged Josephine who didn't move. She nudged her again until her eyes finally opened. "Josie, I'm checking outside. Stay here until I get back. Don't move."

Pauline crawled out from under the bed. Ignoring her sister's request, Josephine followed closely behind. They tiptoed toward the door and Pauline, with a firm grip, slowly opened it. Her heart began to race when she saw her mother's limp body on the floor. She sprinted to her and with trembling hands, gently started to shake her. "Mom, mom." Ada opened her badly bruised eye revealing a deep gash with dried blood. The other eye was swollen shut. Seeing her mother severely battered, Pauline latched onto her neck and started to sob. She knew she needed more help than her pretend nursing this time. Pauline froze when her father strolled in from the kitchen.

"You keep your mouth shut and make sure your big mouth sister does too. Ya got me?" Without looking at her father, Pauline nodded and wiped her tears with her sleeve. "Get your sister and get to school." Pauline didn't want to leave her mother. She threw her arms around her mother's neck again, and held on tight.

Ada whispered into her daughter's ear, "No matter what happens, always know I love you both. Please never forget your education. It's most important."

Harry barked at his daughter, "Now, I said." He yanked her up from the floor, shoving her toward the bedroom. "Get your sister and get out!"

"Let's go, Pauli." Josephine's voice was shaking.

Ada tried desperately to get her daughter to leave the room. She didn't trust her husband's temper. It could flare up at any moment. "Go ahead, Pauline. Just remember what I said about your education."

"I told you last night to forget about that." Harry ran his hand through his hair and started to pace.

Without uttering another sound, Pauline changed into her school clothes. With Josephine by her side, she glanced one last time at her mother and then her father. The visual imprint of her mother lying on the floor was etched into her brain forever.

CHAPTER 2

❦

Judgment Day

After the girls left for school, Harry approached Ada as she gingerly walked from the bathroom. Harry grabbed her arm and said, "Get dressed, I'm bringing you somewhere."

"Where? I'm not going anywhere with you." Ada tried to wrestle her arm free from his grasp, but he was easily able to overpower her.

"I'm taking you to get help."

"Help? I don't need help. You're the one who needs help." Ada wiggled her arm trying to break free. He tightened his grip.

"You need time to think about how you're treating me."

"I'm not going anywhere and leaving my children with you."

"Yes you are. You need to come to your senses." Harry pushed her toward the door. "If you don't do this, the children will be next."

"Don't punish them, they're just kids." Ada dropped to her knees pleading with him.

"Then grab your stuff and let's go."

"How can you do this? They need their mother." Ada sprung to her feet and uncontrollably started pounding on his chest until she collapsed sobbing into her hands. Harry didn't flinch.

"It seems we now have an understanding."

Ada walked reluctantly behind her husband to the front of a large gated entrance. The weathered steel plate, Woodlands, was prominently displayed on the iron gate. Ada followed the sign and scrutinized the barbed wired fence that circled around the perimeter of the property. She couldn't fight him. She had no power and was resigned to her fate. It was the children she worried about.

"What is this?"

"A place you can think about what I said before. Just remember the story. You were beaten by a mugger and fell into a depression."

"I'll only do this if you promise to keep your hands off the girls."

"Don't worry about them. This is only temporary."

"Can I help you?" A guard slowly approached the locked gate. He grumbled, annoyed he had to get up.

"My wife was mugged and badly beaten. I need to get her some help."

The guard glanced over at Ada and softened his gaze when he saw her bruised face. She looked away, blankly staring at the stark, open fields. Having seen the same scenario many times already, the guard didn't ask any questions and opened the gate. Pointing toward one of the smaller buildings at the end of the walkway he said, "Okay. Go to building number five, they'll help you there."

Ada counted twelve buildings in total. Each were four floors high. They started to walk down the stone pathway that connected each building entrance. Open grass fields surrounded the buildings with plenty of benches. Some were occupied.

Hunched over, Ada slowly shuffled behind Harry. Barely able to stand upright, she was emotionally and physically drained. He arrived at the doorway first and stomped back and forth waiting for her. They entered the building together and Harry turned to face her so only she could hear. "Remember what I said, you got mugged." Ada didn't respond. He made sure she heard him and said, "You hear me?" Ada barely acknowledged. He pushed her in front of him.

A lady perked up from behind the counter as soon as she saw them. "Can I help you?"

"Yes, my wife was mugged and badly beaten. I need to check her in so she can get the proper care. I think she's severely depressed from it."

The lady looked at Ada and calmly asked, "Is this the case, ma'am?" Ada didn't answer at first. Harry put his arm around her shoulders and gently squeezed them. They locked eyes. "Ma'am?" Ada turned toward the lady and nodded weakly. Overwhelmed with concern for her little girls, she couldn't hold back her tears any longer. They streamed down her face as she turned away.

"Okay, I need paperwork filled out. Are you signing her in?" Harry reached for the clipboard.

Once he left the institution, Harry strolled down the street thinking about his conversation with Ada, knowing full well he had no intention of ever signing her out. Smirking, he said under his breath, "Yeah right, it's only temporary." Knowing that the girls would be upset, he contemplated how to tell them that their mother was gone. He didn't want to care for them. Instead, he expected his young children to care for him and tend to the household chores.

When he got back to the apartment, he sat at the kitchen table downing whiskey shots while waiting for the girls to come home from school. They were surprised to see their father sitting there when they walked in.

"Where's mommy?" Pauline yelled while frantically running through the apartment.

"She's at a hospital getting help."

"It's all because of you. You hurt her last night!"

"Watch your mouth little girl. I'm your father and you'll be the next one to get a beating if you don't shut up." His anger rose as he poured himself another shot. "Never mind that. Josephine, start sweeping the apartment. Pauline, cook dinner."

"But we have homework."

"I'm not gonna tell ya again. Homework is a waste of time. Start cooking." Harry rubbed his forehead. Josephine didn't understand what was happening. She froze except for the tears welling in her eyes. "I said, now!" Harry slammed the whiskey glass down.

Josephine dashed to the closet and took out a broom. Wiping tears from her eyes, she started to push piles of dust around. In the kitchen, Pauline opened a cabinet drawer to look for a box of matches.

Harry watched as the dust billowed in the air from Josephine's sweeping. He grabbed the broom from her. "This is how you do it. Didn't your mother ever teach ya?" He handed her back the broom. Pauline was busy watching them as she struck a match to light the stove. A dirty towel close to the burner caught fire and quickly burst into flames. Pauline's heart raced as the heat enveloped her. She stood completely still, just staring at the fire.

"What the hell are you doing?" Harry pulled Pauline out of the kitchen and quickly filled a pot with water. He tossed it on the engulfed towel. Turning to face the girls, he shouted, "Get in your room. Now!"

The broom crashed to the floor as the girls raced to their bedroom. Pauline slammed the door shut. "Where's mom, Pauli? I don't want to stay here with dad."

"I don't either. We'll just stay in our room for now."

"Did you lock the door? He scares me."

"I know. Me too." Pauline turned the knob and tested the door to make sure it was locked.

Both girls climbed into the bottom bunk bed together and pulled the covers over their head. Loudly gasping for breath, tears uncontrollably poured down their cheeks.

Harry sat on the couch shooting back more whiskey shots to try and drown out the sound of his sobbing children. His plan had backfired. He realized that he would have to figure something else out.

Eventually they all fell asleep.

The following morning, Harry trudged angrily to work trying to accept that his girls couldn't cook or clean for him. In a fit of fury, he slammed the side of his fist against the vertical post of a large white fence. Stopping to rub his hand, he looked through the rails. Curious, he barreled through the gate and stared at a brick, two-story building with a high, over-arching entryway. He continued walking as he pulled his hat down over his forehead so he wouldn't be easily recognized. White, shuttered windows flanked either side of the long porch. A statue of the Blessed Mary was perched at the base of the stone staircase.

Harry was not a practicing Catholic, but his wife prayed every night with the girls before bedtime. He climbed the steps. Glancing at the large crucifix hanging over the door, he paused to read the inscription underneath, Lodi Orphanage, founded in 1913 by the Sisters of Intention. He thought for a moment. It took him only a second to realize this was his answer. Determined to be freed from all responsibilities, he entered the building.

Hearing the door open, a young woman popped up from behind a desk and stepped out into the hallway. She watched him sluggishly walk through the foyer. She was fully clothed in a nun's habit and only her face was exposed. A long crucifix hung from around her neck and draped down her bosom. Harry stared at the crucifix trying to understand its symbolism. "Hello, I'm Sister Sarah. What brings you here today?"

Looking up at the nun's face he said, "My wife went into a deep depression after being mugged and beaten. I can't care for my two daughters." Sister Sarah made the sign of the cross and looked down in a moment of reflection.

"May God bless your poor wife and give her strength. What kind of person would do that?"

"A very bad one." He looked away from her to avoid eye contact. Sister Sarah noticed his changed demeanor, but didn't press on. After all, the children were her first concern. Founded in Poland in the late 1800s, the Sisters of Intention ministered to orphans, the aged, and the sick. Harry never realized he made a good choice.

"How old are your daughters?"

"Eight and six."

"What a shame for these young girls to lose their mother and father. Not to worry, sir, we will take good care of them while they are here." Sister Sarah handed him a clipboard.

As he filled out the paperwork, Harry rubbed his tear-filled eyes. "I know. I'm heartbroken. But I leave early and come home late and can't give them what they need."

Feeling his burden, Sister Sarah rested her hand on his shoulder. "Don't worry. We'll give them a happy home."

Harry desperately needed a drink when he got home. The first whiskey shot went down too easily, so he immediately chased it with another. Once he started, he couldn't stop. He drank all day and made up his mind to take the girls to the orphanage as soon as they got home from school. He tapped his fingers impatiently on the table and downed another shot of whiskey when he heard the girls talking in the hallway. Pauline and Josephine were deep in conversation when they walked inside. They stopped abruptly when they saw their father. Pauline recognized he was drunk and grabbed her sister's hand.

"Both of you pack your things. You're gonna stay at a place for a while until mom gets out."

"What place?"

"You're just like your mother, always answering back." Harry stood up and stumbled toward Pauline. Steadying himself against the wall, he stopped. "Forget it. Get your stuff. You're both leaving now anyway."

Pauline didn't let it go. "Where? I want to know." Irate, Harry started toward her again. She pulled her sister and they raced passed him to their room. Slamming the door behind her, she turned the lock and pulled at the door a few times to be sure it wouldn't open. Pauline took clothes out of the dresser drawer and placed them on the bed. They didn't have much to pack.

"Where are we going, Pauli?"

"I don't know. But I'm sure it's better than being here with him."

"But, wheeennnn is mom coming back?" Josephine struggled to get the words out over her tears.

Pauline shrugged. "It's just the two of us now. We have to stick together. We're sisters and I'll always protect you."

Pauline packed their belongings into two paper bags, including her treasured book and her sister's doll. All Josephine could do was cry.

"Hurry up, we don't have all day!" Harry screamed as he banged loudly on the door. "If you're not out here by the time I count to three, I'm coming in."

Soon afterward, they trudged down the sidewalk. The young girls carried their paper bags filled with their possessions. Pauline kept a close eye on her father who was stumbling down the street. He led them through the gate and to the front of the orphanage. Harry lifted a bottle hidden in a brown paper bag and took a long swig.

Eager to get away from him, Pauline quickly walked up the steps nudging Josephine to keep up with her. Harry saw that they had quickened their pace and wanted to make sure they memorized the story. "Remember what I told you. If they ask you about mom, she got mugged."

Pauline snapped, "No she didn't, you…"

Suddenly Harry lunged forward reaching for her arm. She turned away before he was able to grab her and he lost his balance. Waving his arms uncontrollably trying to steady himself he yelled, "Yes she did. Do ya wanna wind up in the hospital too?" His face turned very red. Pauline knew not to push it any further and shook her head no.

"I thought so. Now keep your mouth shut. And you, Josephine, do you understand what I said? Your big, fat mouth is always jabbering about." Harry took one final swig from the bottle and chucked the bag into the shrubs on the side of the steps.

They entered the foyer and like before, Sister Sarah immediately appeared in the hallway. She smiled broadly and crouched down to their eye level, opening her arms to give them a hug. "These must be the two angels you told me about earlier." She squeezed both of them at the same time, holding them tight. They were barely able to breathe.

"Here's the nice lady I was telling you about who's gonna take care of you."

Sister Sarah detected Harry's slurred speech and the smell of liquor on his breath. Standing upright, she pulled the children closely next to her. "May the person who did this to your mom be brought to justice."

Pauline glanced at her father. Sister Sarah noticed.

"Yes, I hope so too." Harry walked over to the girls and Sister Sarah watched their interaction closely. He bent down and hugged them. "I'm gonna miss you both so much." He leaned toward Pauline and whispered into her ear. "Remember what I said." Almost falling over, he caught his step, bumping into Sister Sarah as he stood up. He turned, opened his arms wide, and hugged her. "Thank you. Take good care of my girls."

"Don't worry, sir, your two girls are going to be just fine here. You can visit anytime you want."

Harry nodded and left the girls with Sister Sarah. He walked away, never glancing back. The girls stood still. Pauline instinctively grabbed Josephine's hand.

"Come with me girls. I'll show you your room and you can meet some of the other girls." They followed behind Sister Sarah and walked down a long hallway.

Josephine spoke for the first time. "Are there any boys here?"

Sister Sarah chuckled at her innocence. "No, only girls. Right now, we have thirty-four other children in our care."

Pauline was in awe as she walked down the clean and pristine hallway. Shiny, polished dark wood beams accented the painted walls. She didn't see any signs of chipped or peeled paint, mouse traps, dust bunny balls, or dirty windows. It was very clean. The sun started to set and the calming pink hues were a beautiful sight through the crystal clear windows. It was the most beautiful sunset she had ever seen.

Pauline glanced at her sister. She knew she would have to watch over her closely. They both loved their mother dearly. It was all so sudden. Pauline couldn't digest everything that had just happened. If she didn't really understand, how could her sister? In their short lives, Colonial Villa was the only home they knew. And now, it all changed.

This was their first time in a large house. Josephine's eyes were opened wide taking it all in. She looked at every detail as they walked down the long hallway. She remained quiet.

Sister Sarah stopped at a doorway and opened double doors. The girls stepped into a large room. Josephine gasped when she saw rows of beds lined up next to each other. The room was clean, but stark with simple furniture and bedding. Every bed was perfectly made; the frame and linens were all white and identical. A single mattress rested on top of a steel frame with a pillow, one fitted sheet, and a blanket. Pauline quickly counted twenty beds against one wall, and immediately opposite, twenty beds against the other wall. A small crucifix hung above each headboard.

Josephine turned to Sister Sarah. "Where's our room?"

Sister Sarah knelt down to face Josephine. With a soft chuckle she said, "This is where all the girls sleep, together in one room so they can be safely watched over."

"But I usually share bunk beds with my sister. I sleep on the bottom bunk."

Sister Sarah looked at her affectionately and said, "How about you sleep right next to each other here. These will be your beds." She pointed to the two on the end.

Josephine's eyes perked up. "You mean like one big bed?" She ran over to try and push them together.

"No, no, Josephine. You see, we keep each bed under a crucifix so God protects each one of our little angels."

"But my sister protects me from the top bunk." Josephine looked at Pauline.

"Josie, if we sleep next to each other, it's even better. We'll be able to see one another when we talk at night."

Watching and listening to their interaction, Sister Theresa stood in the doorway. As the elder nun, she was the disciplinarian and responsible for running the orphanage. She doled out daily chores and kept the children humbled and obedient. Loudly clearing her throat to get their attention, they turned to look at her. "Where did these two come from, Sister Sarah? Why was I not made aware of them?" Sister Theresa was indifferent to the difficult conversation she had just overheard.

Sister Sarah quickly pulled the beds apart, aligning them back under each crucifix to their proper position. "This is Josephine and Pauline. Their father just dropped them off to us and placed them in our care. I was going to talk to you about them later. Their mother was mugged, badly beaten, and taken to the hospital." Sister Sarah placed her arm around Pauline's shoulder. She wanted to make sure she kept quiet. She was eager to speak to the other nun privately about the situation.

"Yes, we'll talk later. Be sure they know how to make those beds in the morning when they wake up." Sister Theresa turned to leave the room.

Trying not to scare the children any further, Sister Sarah softened her voice. "Girls, every morning when you wake up, you must make your beds. You know how to do that, right?" Pauline nodded yes. Josephine didn't respond, but anxiously looked at her sister.

"Don't worry. I'll help you in the morning," Pauline said.

"Where's everyone?" Josephine asked. She wanted to meet the other girls and play.

"Outside playing," Sister Sarah said. "Let's get your belongings put away first. It will be dinnertime soon. You'll meet the girls then."

It didn't take long to put their meager things away. They didn't have much. However, after seeing the scared look on the girls' faces and the drunken state of their father, Sister Sarah walked between them holding their hands as they entered the dining room for supper. Pauline noticed that it was a small room with five, long, wooden tables arranged in rows, crammed side by side next to each other. Four tables were occupied by children laughing and non-stop talking. Sister Theresa sat with another nun in silence while waiting for Sister Sarah to join them. Dinnertime was at 6:00PM sharp and it was mandatory for everyone to eat all meals together. The only exception was sickness.

Pauline spotted a few girls whispering to each other when they entered the room. She hoped Josephine didn't see them.

"Pauli, why is everyone looking at us?" Josephine grabbed her sister's hand.

"Because you're so pretty." Pauline smiled, nudging her with her shoulder. She sensed they weren't being nice but didn't want to upset Josephine. She had already gone through enough.

Before sitting down, Sister Sarah brought them to get their food. She then walked them to the table where the girls who were whispering sat. "Girls, say hi to Josephine and Pauline. They're staying with us now." Sister Theresa glanced over to watch them interact. All the girls smiled and said hello. Josephine and Pauline placed their plates onto the table before sitting down. They squeezed onto the bench, staying very close to one another. The room fell silent after Sister Theresa clapped her hands three times and rose from her seat to say grace. Famished, the two girls ate without saying another word.

Later that evening, Josephine couldn't wait to play with the other young girls and have some fun. They excitedly raced around the bedroom whacking each other with their pillows. Pauline sat on her bed reading her treasured book. Glancing up to check on her sister, Pauline was glad to see her laughing with the other girls. Josephine stopped for a second to wipe hair away from her eyes and called out to her sister, "Come on, Pauli, have some fun with us." Once her guard was down, one of the other girls struck Josephine right in the head with a pillow and quickly scooted away.

"No, I want to finish reading."

Sprinting to catch the other girl, Josephine didn't hear her sister's reply. Suddenly, Sister Theresa entered the room and clapped her hands three times to get their attention. "This is not recess time. It's bedtime. Get to bed now or you'll get ten strikes with a paddle."

The girls quickly raced toward their beds and got under the covers while Sister Theresa walked up and down each row with her hands clasped in front of her waist. Once the room was completely silent, she unfolded her hands and recited the nighttime prayers.

Pauline peeked at Josephine to make sure she was listening.

CHAPTER 3

Confined to the Institution

Confined to an institution, Ada was overwrought with grief now that she was unable to protect her children. Although she was browbeaten by her husband's physical and emotional abuse, the worry that she carried for her two children was too much to bear. "What will become of them?" she said over and over as she gazed helplessly out her bedroom window. Deep in concentration, she didn't hear the attendant enter the room.

"Are you all right, Ada? You've sat alone all night staring out that window and muttering." The attendant grabbed a blanket and wrapped it around Ada's shoulders. Ada flinched upon feeling the weight of the cloth, but didn't look away from the window as she tugged on it, pulling it more tightly around her. "You haven't touched your lunch or dinner either. You must eat something to get better. I know it's hard, but talking about it helps." Ada nodded to acknowledge the woman. She didn't wish to talk to anyone. Her spirit was broken.

"Okay, if you need anything let me know." The attendant started to walk away observing her patient's despair. She had seen many women like this before and knew it might take some time. She would keep trying though.

"Actually, I have one request," Ada said before the lady left the room. "Would you be kind enough to bring me rosary beads?"

"Of course I will." Surprised to hear her speak for the first time, the attendant sensed a tiny breakthrough. She didn't press on, but wanted to reassure her that she would bring them tomorrow.

The moment the attendant walked out of the room, Ada covered her face with her hands and started sobbing. She reached into her pocket to find her locket and began rubbing it between her fingers for comfort. It was the only physical reminder she had of her children. She opened it, looked at their smiling faces, and was overcome with emotion.

The attendant heard Ada bawling from outside her room and brought her a sedative from the doctor. Ada took it and without wiping away her tears, fell fast asleep.

Ada woke up as soon as the effect of the pill wore off. She could no longer sleep without a sedative. She was heartbroken and needed to know that her daughters were all right. She was so worried about their future. She opened the locket and looked at the girls' photos and began to reminisce about the time she overheard her two children talking while reading a book.

"Pauli, I don't wanna read anymore. It's confusing to me."

"Josie, it's I don't 'want to' read anymore. We have to. We have to learn."

"I'd rather just play. Take my blood pressure again."

Ada was listening in on her children's conversation. She wanted to instill in them the importance of an education and interjected, "Josephine, your studies are important. You must keep reading."

"But mom, it's so boring."

"It will help you in the future. Trust me."

"But I don't want to. Can't we just play instead?"

Upon hearing the front door open, Ada rushed to greet her husband who was arriving home from work. "Harry, I think we need to get Josephine reading lessons."

"Are you nuts? I'm not spending money on that nonsense. Who cares if she has a problem reading?"

"I care."

"Well forget it. It's a waste of money. Just get my dinner ready. I'm hungry." Harry glanced toward the girls. "And you two, put that damn book away and get a broom. Make yourselves useful."

Painfully aware that she could no longer help them prepare for a better future, tears streamed down Ada's cheeks. She was overcome with grief. "What will happen to them?" she said softly. "My poor girls."

CHAPTER 4

Enduring Life in the Orphanage

It was her first night in the orphanage and Pauline was having difficulty falling asleep. She tossed and turned trying to get comfortable. The linens felt rough and stiff against her skin. They were not like the soft, worn sheets she was used to at home. In the darkness, the room was larger than she remembered and she felt exposed and vulnerable without Josephine's bed below her. She realized that Josephine sleeping in the bottom bunk beneath her made her feel safe and protected. Now, things were different.

Pauline was worried for her sister. And for the first time she thought about herself and what had happened to them. The strange room was eerily quiet and she couldn't stop thinking. She rolled over onto her side to look at Josephine but it was too dark to see her. With tears welling up in her eyes she whispered, "Josie, are you still up?" Her sister didn't answer. Pauline turned back over and pulled the sheet up to her chin. She didn't release the covers as tears streamed down her face, wetting the pillow on either side of her head. She didn't bother to wipe them away as she looked up into the dark ceiling. Hoping her mom could intuitively hear her she whispered, "Mom, I miss you." As she stared into the darkness, she drifted off into sleep and dreamed about a promise she made years ago.

Pauline and Ada sat on the couch. Her mother spoke to her very seriously.
"You're the older sister. Always take care of and protect Josephine."

"I will, mom, I promise."

"I'm concerned about her reading. I don't know how she's going to finish school." Ada confided to her older daughter.

"Why won't dad help her with lessons?"

"He doesn't believe in education for girls. He thinks they should cook and clean . . . and take care of men. But you're smarter than that. You'll do more. Always remember two things, your education and your prayers."

"Oh mom, I forgot to say them tonight, can we say them together?"

Pauline got down on her knees and rested her elbows on the couch after making the sign of the cross. Ada joined her daughter. Harry walked in to see his wife and daughter praying. "What's this nonsense?"

"Don't say that in front of Pauline. We're saying our prayers together."

"Forget about that. This apartment needs to get mopped. God can't help you with the mopping," Harry said sarcastically.

"After we finish."

Harry stormed over, grabbed Ada by the arm and yanked her off her knees. "Do it now!" He turned to his daughter to get his point across. "And you, help your mother."

Pauline jolted awake and sat upright in bed. She looked around. It took her a second to recognize her surroundings. Settling down onto her side, she stared into the darkness and cried silently.

Even though it was very late when Pauline finally fell asleep, she woke up early the following morning. The room was quiet and still.

She didn't dare move from the bed, unsure of what to do. Everyone else was peacefully asleep until Sister Theresa walked in and loudly clapped her hands three times. "Time to get up. Time for breakfast. Time for chores. Let's go girls," she said. No one moved. Pauline stayed completely still waiting for one of the other girls to get up first. Josephine was still in a deep sleep, she could hear her breathing heavily. "Now! Or the paddle comes out," Sister Theresa said sternly.

The girls quickly sprang out of bed. They raced to change their clothes and headed toward the door. Pauline joined the pack but noticed that Josephine was still asleep, unaware of the commotion going on in the room. She quickly darted back to her bed and shook her to wake up. She didn't move. She pulled her arm and said, "Come on, Josie, you have to get up now."

Sister Theresa approached the bed. "I see we have a sleepyhead on our hands."

"No, Sister. She's just really tired from all that's happened over the last few days." Pauline pulled Josephine out of the bed pleading with her, "Josie, come on, we have to go now." Slowly, Josephine got her footing as she rubbed her tired eyes. She staggered trying to follow her older sister.

"Where are we going this time? I just want to sleep some more."

"I know, but it's time to get up. We have to eat and do our chores."

"Chores? What chores?"

"I don't know. We'll find out soon."

The girls followed the group into the dining room and waited on the back of the line to get their breakfast. Pauline looked around for Sister Sarah. She felt lost and really wanted to talk to her. As they approached the serving table, they picked up a bowl of oatmeal, buttered toast, and milk. They sat at the same table as the night before. Josephine looked down at her food and said, "I don't like oatmeal. Can I have something else?"

"No. You have to eat it. We won't get anything else to eat until lunch. Make sure you finish it all."

Sister Theresa clapped her hands three times loudly. Everyone stopped talking and looked up at her. "Let's say our morning prayers now."

After prayers, all the girls ate except for Josephine. A young girl at the table noticed and urged her on. "We need to start chores before school starts. Eat up quickly, there isn't much time."

"Come on. I know you don't like it, but it's all we will get. You have to eat." Pauline pleaded with her younger sister.

Sister Theresa slowly and deliberately, with her hands clasped behind her back, started to walk toward Josephine. Josephine panicked when she saw the nun walking in her direction and began shoveling the oatmeal into her mouth. She kept her head down until she finished it all. "Pauline and Josephine, come see me when you're done." Josephine heard the stern voice, but never looked up.

Uncertain what to expect from the older nun, Pauline and Josephine stayed very close to each other and kept bumping into one another as they walked toward Sister Theresa. Once again, Pauline tried to get Sister Sarah's attention. She wanted desperately to talk to her. Sister Sarah didn't notice.

"Pauline, you'll help the cook." Sister Theresa pointed toward the kitchen door. "Go to her now, she's expecting you. Josephine, come with me."

Josephine apprehensively followed the nun out of the room. She kept glancing back at Pauline, nervous to be alone with Sister Theresa. Pauline was worried for her sister. This was the first time they had been separated since they arrived at the orphanage. Josephine hurried behind Sister Theresa and struggled to keep up with her pace as they walked down the long corridor to the community bathroom. Josephine was afraid to speak but glad to see another young girl in the bathroom. She didn't want to be alone with Sister Theresa for another minute. "Help her scrub the floor. The brushes are in the closet over there. Later, follow her to the schoolroom when it's time for your studies. I'll be checking in on you so keep to your work and no playing around." Sister Theresa sternly addressed Josephine and left the room.

Once the nun was out of sight, Josephine sighed and glanced toward the other young girl who was on her hands and knees scrubbing the floor. The young girl didn't look up or deviate from her task. She just kept scrubbing. Josephine got a brush from the closet, bent down, and copied the girl's routine. After a short while in silence, Josephine wiped the sweat from her forehead and said, "How long do we do this for?" The young girl looked up at Josephine, darted her eyes to look at the doorway, but quickly went back to work without responding. She was afraid Sister Theresa was listening outside the door.

It was a long time before the young girl finally spoke. "Let's go, it's time for our studies." She stood up, emptied the bucket, then rinsed and placed the brush in the closet to dry. Josephine quickly cleaned her brush just like the other girl. As Sister Theresa instructed, she followed her to the schoolroom. Neither one spoke.

Pauline was already in the schoolroom anxiously waiting for her sister to arrive. She kept glancing at the doorway in anticipation. As soon as Josephine entered the room, Pauline ran over to her. "Are you okay?"

"Yes. I was scrubbing the bathroom floor with that girl." Josephine pointed to a girl who sat in the corner. "She wouldn't talk to me. She was very nervous. Sister Theresa said she was going to come back but she never did. Where were you?"

"I was in the kitchen peeling potatoes with the cook. She didn't stop talking."

The girls broke out into laughter as Sister Sarah entered the schoolroom. "Okay girls, settle down. There will be time for laughter later during recess. Now, it's time to study." Josephine rolled her eyes and settled down into a desk next to Pauline.

Later during recess, Josephine played outside with the other girls. She was having a great time singing songs, playing hopscotch, and jumping rope. She couldn't have been happier. Pauline, on the other hand, didn't want to play with the girls and wandered back inside to look for Sister Sarah. She peeked into the schoolroom first, but found her in the front office sitting by a desk tending to paperwork. Pauline quietly walked inside. "Good afternoon, Sister Sarah."

"Pauline!" The young nun was surprised to see her. "How come you're not outside playing with the other girls?"

"If it's okay, can I sit here and read a book?"

"Of course, my dear, but wouldn't you rather be outside playing and having some fun?"

"I really don't like playing those games. I like to read in my spare time." Sister Sarah walked over to a shelf where a few dusty books rested.

She pulled one down and handed it to her. "We don't have many books, but here's one you might like."

"Thank you." Pauline couldn't wait. She quickly opened the book to start reading, but Sister Sarah probed further.

"What games do you like to play?"

"I like playing pretend nurse. Josephine pretends she's the patient, but she really prefers playing outside with the girls. With everything that she's gone through, she should play with them."

"Oh yes, your sister told me you want to be a nurse."

Pauline's face lit up as she spoke. "That's always been a dream of mine." Her enthusiasm waned as she continued. "But it will never happen. I won't have the money for college."

"Pauline, my dear, you can have anything in this world you put your heart and mind to. Nothing can stop you from attaining your dreams."

Sister Sarah opened a drawer and pulled out a packet of papers. She handed her an application. "You hold onto this. When the time comes, you apply here. It's the best nursing school in the area."

Pauline looked across the top of the paper: The Intention Nursing Program, New Rochelle, New York. "What's this?"

"It's a Catholic women's college in New York founded by the Sisters of Intention. You're a good student. That school is exactly what you're looking for."

Curiously, she started to read the paper. She couldn't stop smiling.

Living in the orphanage was an adjustment for the two young girls. As they settled into a routine of set schedules and disciplined chores, they longed for family time and the closeness they once shared with their mother. Every night, the two girls chatted in bed after the lights were out. They talked about everything and never kept secrets from one another. However, in all their conversations, they never once mentioned their father. Facing each other in the darkness, they whispered so the other girls couldn't hear.

"I hate this place. I can't wait to get out of here. All we do are chores and school work," Josephine said.

"I know. Hopefully, we'll be the next ones to get adopted." Pauline often dreamed of a nice couple taking them in and having enough money to send her to nursing school.

"I hope soon. I mean, why did this happen to us? A lot of the other girls have already been adopted. How come we haven't been?"

"I don't know. At least we have each other. I guess it's how our lives are supposed to be."

"I guess so, but I'm tired of scrubbing floors. We better get some sleep before the clapping starts." Josephine giggled, but quickly covered her mouth to keep it quiet.

Pauline chuckled at her sister's reaction. "Good night, Josie."

"Good night, Pauli."

Josephine was a sound sleeper and quickly fell asleep after their talks. However, Pauline continued to have trouble sleeping and often sat on the edge of the bed staring out the window into the darkness. The moon and stars illuminated the sky. They reminded her of all life's possibilities. She was determined to find a way to go to nursing school. Although she was already tormented about the possibility of having to leave her sister, just thinking about becoming a nurse made her giddy. She reached under her pillow for the application Sister Sarah had given her. She kept it close by to remind herself of the opportunity.

It was a beautiful, sunny day. At recess all the girls, except for Pauline, dashed outdoors to play. They couldn't wait to get outside. Pauline sat in the corner chair in the front office and read, retreating to a safe haven inside the pages of her book. She was buried in the latest adventure when Sister Sarah walked in. The nun was looking for Pauline to share some news, possibly life changing news, that she had uncovered earlier that day.

Hesitating a moment before speaking, Sister Sarah stood watching her. She wanted to make sure she had the right words. "Pauline."

Pauline looked up. "Oh hi, Sister Sarah. I didn't know you were there."

"I have something to ask you."

Pauline earmarked the page and closed the book to give the nun her full attention.

"I looked over the application your father submitted. Do you know you have an aunt?"

"No. My mother never mentioned her."

Sister Sarah was surprised that her mother never spoke about a close relative. She wondered if there was something wrong with her aunt and decided to continue cautiously. "Well, she's your father's sister. She lives in New York close to the nursing school. Are you sure your parents never mentioned her?"

"Yes, I'm sure. I have no idea who she is."

"I see."

"Did it say where my mother is?"

"No dear, your father left that part of the application blank."

The conversation abruptly ended when they heard the front door to the orphanage open. A young couple entered the foyer. Pauline sat quietly while Sister Sarah stepped into the hallway to greet them. The man wore a well–tailored suit and removed his fedora the moment he saw the nun. Pauline's mouth opened wide when the woman strutted down the hallway in a cloche hat wearing the most beautiful silk-crepe, drop-waisted dress she had ever seen.

"Can I help you?" Sister Sarah asked.

"Yes. My husband and I desperately want a child to raise as our own. We're looking to adopt a young girl." Pauline stirred in the chair leaning forward to hear the whole conversation.

"May God bless you. Do you have an age preference?"

"We don't have much money, but we will raise the girl with a good home life and lots of love. We're hoping to find a bright girl. Schooling is very important to us and we'll make sure she gets a good education."

The nun brought them into the office. Pauline's eyes widened in panic. Catching Sister Sarah's glance, she sat on the edge of her chair shaking her head vehemently no. Ignoring her actions, Sister Sarah motioned her hand in Pauline's direction. "This is Pauline. She's the brightest one of the bunch. She has a passion to be a nurse." The lady glanced toward Pauline and smiled. "She has a younger sister. I would ask you to consider taking both of them." Relieved, Pauline sat back in her chair. She couldn't leave Josephine, it was too soon to separate.

The lady looked at her husband and said, "Can we afford both of them?"

"Is she a good student too?" the man asked.

"She tries hard but she's, well…full of life, perky, and lots of fun. You would love her."

He shook his head no. "We're only able to adopt one." Pauline looked down. Sister Sarah noticed her disappointment.

"I'm sorry. I don't have the heart to split them up. But, since Pauline is here, why don't we ask her directly." Sister Sarah nodded at Pauline.

"Thank you, but I can't leave my sister. She's too young and we only have each other."

"You're a special young girl for thinking of your sister in that way," the lady said.

"Yes, she is special. She is definitely very special," Sister Sarah repeated.

Pauline politely excused herself. She suddenly had a strong urge to see her sister who was outside playing with the other girls. Pauline sat on a bench and watched the young girls run around each other laughing and enjoying recess. Josephine, always bubbly and full of life, was in the middle of all the commotion. Josephine was surprised to see her sister outside and called out, "Come on, Pauli, play with us and have some fun for once. Don't just sit there."

Sister Theresa entered the playground and approached Margie. As the two youngest girls, Margie and Josephine often played together and immediately stopped running when they spotted the nun. "Margie, come and say your goodbyes. A young family has decided to give you a home." Josephine gasped and dropped her head in disappointment. "Go inside and pack your bag. They're waiting for you with Sister Sarah." Sister Theresa turned away from the girls to enter the building.

Josephine hung her head low and climbed on the bench next to her sister. "All our friends are leaving. How come no one takes us?"

"I don't know, Josie." She couldn't tell her sister the truth. She would be crushed.

THE LOOMING RECESSION
1929

CHAPTER 5

❦

The End of A Decade

It was 1929. Three years had passed since the girls entered the orphanage. Pauline was now eleven. She accepted the daily routine and constant chores doled out by Sister Theresa. As the worrier, Pauline was certain they would never get adopted together. They were destined to make it on their own somehow.

At nine years old, Josephine hated the predictability, and most of all, the disciplined studying. She continued to struggle with her lot in life. She tried hard to forget her father and all the hurt he had caused. She never spoke about him but in suppressing his memory, he surfaced in a recurring dream about the last beating she witnessed. In the vivid recollection, her father's stern voice was yelling at them all, her mother's piercing screams echoed after the clap of a belt, and the close up image of a beaten and bruised face from her father's torment usually jolted her awake. It was the same dream each time. She awoke crying many nights and never told anyone, not even Pauline. She also tried to stay far away from Sister Theresa. The elder nun wasn't violent but she was stern, intimidating, and demanding. She was always ordering Josephine to do something—scrub the floor, wake up, go to sleep, make your bed, read, study, clean the table. In many ways, she was just like Josephine's father.

Over the last few years, Sister Sarah had watched over the girls, but developed an exceptionally close bond with Pauline. Similar to their mother, Sister Sarah knew Pauline was a bright student. She always encouraged her to keep up with her studies and to never lose sight of her dream of becoming a nurse. Even though it was unconfirmed, the nun suspected they had an abusive father and knew she couldn't protect them forever. But, while they were in the orphanage and under her care, she would do everything she could to keep them safe.

However, a sudden turn of events forced unexpected changes that affected everyone. It was October 29, 1929, and a typical day for most. The girls played outside while Pauline quietly read in the front office. Sister Sarah hurried in startling Pauline, causing her to look up from her book. Pauline watched the nun fumble for the knob to turn up the volume on the radio as they listened to a somber announcement.

"Folks, this is the worst day in history. Investors are losing their fortunes. The stock market has plummeted. This could have a serious financial impact on our economy. May God be with us all."

Sister Sarah turned the radio off and stared out the window in silence with her hands clasped. Confused by what she just heard, Pauline said, "What does that mean?"

"We rely heavily on donations and gifts. This could be devastating." Sister Sarah bowed her head in reflection and made the sign of the cross.

"I don't understand." Pauline was trying to make sense of it all.

"The stock market is where people invest to try and make more money. It's a gamble though. Sometimes people make a lot and other times they lose a lot. It just crashed, so everyone is losing. If people don't have money, they can't donate."

"Why would anyone do it then? Why would people want to lose money?"

"They don't expect to lose money. They just want more of it. It's called greed, Pauline, it's one of the seven deadly sins." Sister Sarah explained further. "The twenties were an economic boost for many. People had plenty of money to spend. This drastic decline will affect them, and as a result, greatly impact us."

Later that evening when the children were asleep, Sister Sarah and Sister Theresa paced in their upstairs quarters worried about the economic impact on the orphanage. "Sister Sarah, I'm concerned for the children." Sister Theresa spoke first. "This could shut us down for good. We are barely able to get by now and we can't ask the girls to do anymore chores. They're only children." Her voice trailed off as she continued to pace. Sister Sarah was surprised by the older nun's compassion since Sister Theresa had always been so stern with the girls. Sister Sarah wondered if their financial situation was more serious than what she knew.

Not letting her concern show, Sister Sarah said, "Let's just see how it goes. Maybe the market will come back and all the worry will be forgotten."

"We can't wait. It's worse than we know." Sister Theresa felt the weight of her responsibilities. "It's reported that people are taking their own lives, tragically jumping out of buildings because they've lost so much. It's dreadful." In unison, each nun reached for the crucifix that hung around her neck and prayed. Sister Theresa broke the silence. "We will start cutting back immediately."

"On what? We…the children have so little already."

"We'll talk to the cook in the morning. We'll start rationing the food."

"Rationing the food? They're children, isn't there another way?"

"I don't think so. Let's pray on it this evening. We'll talk to the cook tomorrow."

The following morning, Pauline was daydreaming while waiting on line to get her breakfast. If people don't have money, they can't donate. She intently thought about Sister Sarah's words and wasn't paying attention to her younger sister who held a bowl with a small scoop of porridge. Josephine wanted more and didn't move. Sister Theresa looked at Josephine. "Is there a problem, young lady, you're holding up the line?"

"No, Sister Theresa. It's just that I'm hungry and wanted more than one scoop," Josephine softly replied.

"That's all you're getting today, so don't leave anything behind. Eat it all up." Sister Theresa folded her hands together and walked away.

"All day?" Josephine raised her voice so Sister Theresa could hear her. She turned to her sister hoping to get an answer. "Pauli, why aren't we getting any food today?"

Startled by her little sister's outburst Pauline asked, "Josie, what's going on? Why are you raising your voice?"

"I'm hungry and this is all we're getting to eat today." Josephine tilted the bowl to show her sister.

Sister Theresa heard Josephine's outburst and turned around to address her. Taking a few steps to get closer to Josephine she said, "I know you're hungry, Josephine, we're all hungry. You're too young to understand. One day you will. For now, one scoop a day is all you're getting."

"Pauli, I don't understand?"

Pauline nudged her to move along. "Let's go sit down. There's something big happening that even I don't understand. Eat it all and don't waste a drop."

THE ECONOMIC DEPRESSION
1930s

CHAPTER 6

❦

The Declining Economy

The economy was worse than expected. It was 1932, three years after the crash and the orphanage was overrun with girls and severely overcrowded. The number of desperate, out-of-work people who could no longer care for their children escalated as the economy declined. Fearing they would be turned away if they entered the building, parents left children alone on the front steps hoping they would be found and taken care of by the generosity of the Sisters of Intention. Sister Sarah brought each child inside. She couldn't turn them away even though there wasn't enough food or beds to accommodate the influx of girls. Children were forced to sleep on the floor with only a blanket to soften their bodies against the hard ground. Young, smaller children shared a bed. To make matters worse, the declining economy halted adoptions. Not one child was taken in by a family in over three years. People were scared. There wasn't any money. It was exactly what Sister Theresa had feared.

In order to make room in the bedroom for the other children, Pauline and Josephine's beds were butted up next to each other now, just the way Josephine originally wanted it. She loved being close to her sister at night. She was having fewer nightmares now. It also made their nighttime talks easier.

"Pauli, how much longer do you think until we get more food? My clothes don't fit anymore and I have to keep pinning the waist so they don't fall down."

"I'm not sure, maybe never. New kids are being dropped off every day now. Look at this place."

"We're the oldest, so we'll never be adopted, right?"

"I don't think so. We'll soon be leaving here to be on our own. We can't stay forever."

"Where would we go?"

"I don't know, Josie, I don't know."

CHAPTER 7

Pauline's Time Is Now

It was 1936 and ten years had passed since the girls entered the orphanage. The country still suffered from an economic depression and food, jobs, and necessities were scarce. Even so, at eighteen years old, Pauline was ready to pursue her lifelong dream of becoming a nurse. She thought often about the tough road she had ahead. She didn't have a well thought out plan yet, but was determined to find her way in the world outside the orphanage. Pauline confided to Josephine her intention. Although she was heartbroken, Josephine supported her decision and didn't want to hold her sister back any longer. It was time.

It was early morning and Pauline was in bed thinking about her future. She wondered how she could be both excited and scared at the same time when, like every other morning, Sister Theresa walked in the bedroom and loudly clapped her hands three times. "It's time to get up, girls. Let's go."

Pauline and Josephine rolled off their beds. Josephine turned to her sister and said, "I'm not going to miss that when I leave." She started to chuckle and didn't watch where she was going. She stepped on a girl who was still sleeping on the floor and unresponsive to Sister Theresa's obnoxious clapping. Josephine lost her balance and tumbled onto her. Laughing loudly and struggling to stand up, she remembered how she hated getting out of bed when she first arrived. She woke the young girl up, just like Pauline usually had to wake her up before the nun appeared at her bedside. Thankfully for the new arrivals, there were too many girls piled in the room for Sister Theresa to notice.

"I'm going to miss you so much, Pauli," Josephine said as she finally regained her composure. "You've grown into such a pretty and tall young lady." She teased.

Pauline looked at her grown-up, younger sister. She was much slimmer now from the food shortage, but Pauline had noticed for a while, that Josephine had matured and no longer complained as much. She was still a fun loving and jovial soul at heart but her sweet innocence was gone. She had changed so much. Pauline had protected her as much as she could, but their hardships were too great. She couldn't protect her from everything and the economic depression took its toll on everyone. "And you, my sweet, little sister, what am I going to do without you?"

"You know, we've been here for ten years and I think I've scrubbed the bathroom floor 3,650 times by now. I know every detail of every tile." Pauline smiled, pleased that her math was correct. Josephine didn't notice and continued talking. "You're so lucky you're leaving."

"I hate leaving you. We've never been apart. Plus, I promised mom I would always protect you."

"You have to go to that nursing school you applied to. That's your dream." Josephine always rooted for her sister. "Did you find out yet if you've been accepted?"

"Not yet." Pauline downplayed her uneasiness. "I probably won't get accepted anyway."

"Don't say that!" Josephine looked right at her. "You're the smartest person I know. You'll definitely get in."

Pauline nodded to her sister but didn't say anything. As if reading her mind, Josephine lightened the mood. "I gotta go do my morning chores before Sister Theresa comes back. Here I go on my hands and knees again." Josephine hugged her before walking away.

Sister Sarah watched the interaction between the two sisters from a distance. She knew how close they were and suspected Josephine would have a hard time staying behind without Pauline. Once Josephine started to head down the hallway, Sister Sarah approached Pauline. "Can I see you in the office please? I have something I would like to give you."

They walked silently toward the front office. Pauline was still thinking about her discussion with Josephine. It broke Pauline's heart that she would be leaving without her. Upon entering the office, Sister Sarah picked up a piece of paper and couldn't contain her happiness. She smiled broadly and exclaimed, "You did it. Congratulations!" She embraced Pauline, holding her tight.

"Did what?"

"You got accepted. I always knew you would." Sister Sarah handed her a letter.

Pauline quickly scanned the paper to be absolutely sure. A rare, broad smile lit up her face when she finally looked up. "I don't believe it," she said. "I'm really going." And then suddenly, her smile diminished.

"Pauline, what's wrong? Isn't this what you always wanted?"

"I'm happy, but how am I going to leave Josie?"

"We'll take care of your sister until she is ready to leave here. I promise." Sister Sarah grabbed her by both arms to reassure her. "You have to do this for yourself. It's a joyous time, be happy. It's your calling and God has answered your prayers. Josephine wouldn't want you to stay."

Pauline knew she was right.

After Pauline left, Sister Sarah held onto her crucifix and started pacing. She hoped the letter she sent to Pauline's Aunt Bertha arrived. She suspected Pauline would be leaving very soon now and hadn't heard back from her aunt yet.

Dear Bertha,

My name is Sister Sarah from Lodi Orphanage in Lodi, New Jersey. We have been caring for your two nieces, Josephine and Pauline, for ten years now. The girls don't know I am writing, but Pauline has a passion to be a nurse and would like to attend a nursing school in New Rochelle. She's close to eighteen years old now and will soon be leaving us. She desperately wants to attend the nursing school. Would you be so kind to find it in your heart and take her in so she can follow her dream? She's a great girl.

God Bless.

Sincerely,

Sister Sarah

Aunt Bertha read the pristine handwritten letter a few times. She rested the palm of her hand against her drawn and weathered face and stared into the emptiness of her small apartment. Two nieces? Orphanage? What the hell has Harry been up to? She sat staring at the letter while tapping her fingers against the table. She lit her cigarette, gulped down the rest of her beer, and began to scheme.

Pauline spent the following week preparing for her trip to New Rochelle. Even though she knew her aunt had responded to Sister Sarah's letter and agreed to take her in, it was the night before her long journey and still, she couldn't sleep. She was confident that it was time to finally follow her dream, but her heart pounded and mind raced all night long with thoughts of the unknown. It was bittersweet. The following morning, she stood with Josephine and Sister Sarah on the sidewalk in front of the gate. They stayed together for a long time. Josephine swayed back and forth trying to delay the inevitable. No one wanted to be the first to say goodbye. Sister Sarah broke the awkwardness and reached for Pauline, drawing her in tight. Choking back tears she said, "You're a special girl, Pauline. The world is yours to take." Releasing her from her hold, Sister Sarah handed Pauline and envelope. "Here's the money I promised. It's not much, but will help get you started."

"Thank you for everything you've done for me." Pauline's eyes started to fill up with tears at the thought of leaving her.

Sister Sarah tucked a piece of paper into Pauline's hand. "And here's your aunt's address. The good news is she sounded very receptive. Stay with her until you can get settled."

Pauline scanned the letter before putting it inside her coat pocket. "I can't thank you enough. I'll really miss you." This time Pauline reached out to hug her only friend from the orphanage. Sister Sarah walked away to give the girls some privacy.

Unable to hold back her tears any longer, Josephine's face was already wet. She threw her arms around her sister and almost knocked her over. Squeezing her tight, she rested her head on her older sister's shoulder and exclaimed, "My sister's gonna be a nurse!"

Pauline corrected her and said, "Going to be." They both exploded into laughter, but still held onto each other and couldn't let go. They had been together for sixteen years and didn't want to be separated now. Through every hardship, they were the only constant in each other's lives. Reluctantly, Pauline broke away from her sister's embrace. She bent down to pick up her life's possessions that fit in one small bag. "I'll write you as soon as I can." Facing the sidewalk, she stared for a long moment down the street. She couldn't move.

"Don't be afraid, Pauline, God is with you." Sister Sarah reassured her. Pauline took a deep breath, raised her head up high, and began to walk down the street to the bus depot. Tears streamed down her face as she walked toward the unknown. Uncertain and scared for herself, she was even more worried for her sister.

Sister Sarah and Josephine stood together watching her walk away. Josephine grabbed the nun's hand as they silently cried together. They didn't move until they could no longer see Pauline's figure in the distance. Then together, still holding hands, they went back inside without saying a word.

⌒⌒

CHAPTER 8

A New World Awaits

Walking along the street, Pauline easily found the bus depot a few miles down the road. She was already exhausted and glad she spent the prior week planning her travels so she knew exactly where to go.

Pauline sat in the front seat of the bus and stared out the window during the long trip from New Jersey to New York City. As far as she could remember, this was her first time outside of Lodi. In fact, for the last ten years, she rarely went outside the orphanage. She took in all the sights from the open fields along the highway to the busy streets of New York City. Walking from the NYC Bus Depot to Grand Central Station, she constantly looked up at the skyscrapers. The enormously tall buildings captivated her. She was overwhelmed by the number of people physically in one place. It was exhilarating and frightening at the same time. When she finally arrived at Grand Central Station, she thought about her sister and wished she could have brought her along. She knew Josephine would have loved it. Pauline sat in the front of the train and reread the paper Sister Sarah handed her with her aunt's address. She noticed a nice looking man in uniform pass by. "Excuse me sir, do you work on this train?"

"Why yes, ma'am. What can I do for you?"

"I want to make sure I'm going the right way. Will this train take me to Franklin Avenue in New Rochelle?"

"Yes, ma'am. This train stops in New Rochelle. I'm not sure exactly where Franklin Avenue is but you'll be a lot closer than you are now." He smiled politely.

"I see. Thank you, sir."

He tipped his cap and nodded. "We'll be leaving in just a few minutes. Enjoy the ride."

During the long ride, Pauline stared out the window. When she saw the unfamiliar land and buildings whizzing by, she realized how far away she had traveled from the orphanage. She was grateful that Sister Sarah had contacted her aunt. When the train finally arrived in New Rochelle, she paused before stepping onto the platform. At that moment she realized her whole life was about to change. She took a deep breath, lifted her head up high, picked up her bag, wrapped her coat tightly around her, and stepped into her new life.

Despite her brave approach, she quickly became flustered as she glanced around unsure of the direction to her aunt's house. She spotted a police officer standing on the corner and hurried over to him.

"Excuse me, sir, could you please tell me where Franklin Avenue is?"

"It's over in that direction." He pointed northeast. "Go one block east, then two blocks north."

"Thank you." Pauline scurried away following his directions.

It was exactly where he said and once she arrived at the address, Pauline paused in front of a brick stand-alone building. The wooden fence needed a fresh coat of white paint and the overgrown grass a good cutting. Not only was the building run-down looking, it was smaller than she expected. She held her bag tighter as she climbed the stairs to the front door. Pauline had many questions she hoped her aunt would answer. She specifically wanted to know why her aunt hadn't taken them in when they were young. Sister Sarah said her aunt sounded nice in the letter. Pauline hoped she was right. Taking a deep breath, she knocked on the door. A moment later, the door opened. Pauline was shocked to see that her aunt appeared wrinkled and thin. She was wearing old, poorly-fitted clothes. Smiling, Aunt Bertha was genuinely pleased to see her niece and said, "My God, you're beautiful, Pauline." She pulled her in to hug her. Pauline didn't know how to respond and stood very stiff. Her only adult interaction had been with her parents and the nuns in the orphanage. Sister Theresa certainly didn't show any affection toward her.

"Come on in."

Exhausted from the day of traveling, Pauline followed her aunt dragging her body up three flights of stairs. Pauline looked around. "You don't live in a house?"

"I did, but when your uncle died, I put the money into the stock market. When the market crashed, I lost it all and was forced to sell the house. I couldn't afford it any longer. Never make that mistake." She glared at Pauline and then suddenly threw her head back and diabolically broke out into laughter. Pauline stepped away from her aunt alarmed by her sudden outburst. Her hysteria only lasted a moment though. With a straight face Aunt Bertha calmly said, "Where's all your stuff?"

Pauline lifted the small bag. "It's all here."

Startled, her aunt looked down. "That's all you have?" Pauline nodded and followed her aunt into a small, messy living room. Empty beer cans were piled high and cigarette butts covered a coffee table. She glanced around the dark, dreary room. There was an old couch with a stain on the cushion, dark curtains that prevented the sunshine from entering the room, and a small lamp on a wood table. Aunt Bertha noticed Pauline looking around the room and said, "It's not much. Only a one bedroom so you'll have to sleep on the couch."

"Thank you for doing this. I'll find my own place as soon as I can."

"Well, until then." Aunt Bertha handed her a piece of paper. "These are your chores."

"Chores?" Pauline was stunned.

Hysterically laughing again, Aunt Bertha snapped, "Everyone has to earn their keep. There are no freebies in this world."

Pauline let out an audible sigh. She cleared the coffee table while her aunt looked on. It wasn't quite the welcome she had expected.

Later that evening, Pauline was awake on the couch wondering what she had gotten into. Her body ached from the long day of traveling while her mind kept rehashing her aunt's crazy and demanding behavior. The stale smell of cigarettes and beer permeated her senses. Suddenly realizing she forgot to say her prayers, she stood up and knelt beside the couch. Making the sign of the cross, she placed her hands in the prayer position, closed her eyes tightly as she bowed her head down. "Please God, watch over my sister and me. Give us the strength to move on. Amen."

CHAPTER 9

A Determined Spirit

The following morning, Pauline was eager to find the nursing school. She couldn't wait to start her classes. With hardly a night's rest, she left the apartment early to walk to Main Street, the local mecca for shopping, business, and eateries. Ironically, she spotted the same police officer from the day before. "Good morning, sir, can you tell me how to get to the Intention Nursing School?"

The police officer instantly recognized her. "Good morning, ma'am. I take it you found Franklin Avenue?"

Surprised that he remembered Pauline replied, "Yes, sir, it's right where you said."

The officer smiled. "Okay, now to the Intention Nursing School. Here's what you do. Walk to the bus depot a quarter mile down. Get off the bus at Division Street and you'll see the big building on your left. Walk four street blocks to get to the main entrance."

"Thank you, but I would like to walk."

"Walk? It's not close." Taken by surprise, the officer shrugged his shoulders before giving her new directions. "Well, the easy way is to go about one and one-half miles down North Avenue and turn left on Lockwood. It's about a quarter mile down the road from there. Good luck."

"Thank you." Pauline practically skipped the whole way to the school. Excited that her dream was finally coming true, she couldn't wait to get there.

Upon arriving at the college, she paused in front of the stone building and saw a sign with Intention Nursing School written in big bold letters. She read it a few times just to make sure she was really there. She took a deep breath, opened the front door, and entered the lobby. As she approached the front desk, a young lady heard her coming and looked up from her magazine. "Can I help you?"

"Yes, I'm looking for admissions."

"Sure, second door on the right." The young lady immediately went back to reading.

Pauline walked down the stark and bare hallway toward the admissions office. With each sound of her footsteps, she knew she was one step closer to her dream. She paused at the door to savor the moment, then confidently entered the room. A middle-aged nun was sitting at a desk watching Pauline charge through the door.

"Hi, my name is Pauline."

The nun immediately interjected, "Roka?"

Surprised by the interruption, Pauline self-consciously responded, "Yes, how did you know?"

"We've been expecting you, dear. Sister Sarah from the Lodi Orphanage wrote to us. I'm Sister Margaret. Have a seat, please." Pauline sat across from the nun who was diligently looking over her application. Pauline settled into her seat and immediately noticed that Sister Margaret was wearing the same style habit as the nuns in the orphanage. Pauline grew hopeful that Sister Margaret would become an ally like Sister Sarah had been. After Sister Margaret flipped the last page she smiled at Pauline. "I have to say, your records are exceptional. So tell me, why do you want to become a nurse?"

Pauline paused, unsure of what to say. Looking down to gather her thoughts, she was suddenly overcome with emotion. She started to cry thinking about how proud her mother would be of this moment. The nun reached for Pauline's hand and softly said, "It's okay. You don't have to be nervous."

"It's not that. I spent many nights helping my mother."

"That's a good thing. You should be proud you helped your mother with household chores."

"No. I was icing the bruises and whip marks she got from my father. It was then I knew I wanted to become a nurse. She encouraged me to always follow my dream."

"I see. May God be with you my child. Is your mother still alive?"

"I don't know. I haven't seen her since my father left me at the orphanage when I was eight."

"Didn't your parents ever visit you?"

"No, never."

Sister Margaret looked down knowing she was going to gravely disappoint this young lady. The nun sensed that Pauline had already gone through so much. Softening her gaze, Sister Margaret said, "I did the best I could with the tuition. Unfortunately, the donations have been drastically reduced because of the economy."

Pauline sat straight in the chair and leaned closer to the nun. "I'm sorry. I don't know what that means."

"Until our donations pick back up, you would have to pay a large amount of the tuition."

"But I don't have a job." Pauline's voice started to shake.

"I'm sorry, we just don't have any more money right now to offer you. The depression really hurt us." Sister Margaret looked away. She knew Pauline didn't have the money or resources to go to college. It broke her heart to deliver this news.

Pauline understood. She lived through it first hand while at the orphanage. "I see. I'll be back once I get a job. Please, don't give my spot away."

Surprised by her will and determination Sister Margaret said, "You will always be welcome here, my dear. Never lose faith."

"I won't, it's what brought me to you in the first place." Pauline rose to leave.

Sister Margaret knew standing before her was a young woman who one day would realize her dream and become a nurse. She was confident she would see her again as she watched Pauline march out of the room.

CHAPTER 10

✑

Hope

While in the institution, Ada sat alone and gazed out her bedroom window. Drawn and extremely frail, she moved her fingers to the next bead and mumbled prayers to herself. Every day was the same.

The attendant walked in and wrapped a blanket around Ada's shoulders. It was a nightly ritual. Unexpectedly, Ada reached back and held her hand. The attendant was surprised by Ada's uncharacteristic gesture. They rarely exchanged words, they certainly weren't affectionate with each other. "You're a kind young lady. I'll never forget how good you've been to me." Ada turned to look at her.

"Do you think your husband will ever sign you out?" the attendant asked trying to engage her in conversation.

"No, never. I've been here too long. He's not a good man." Ada returned her gaze to the window.

"I'm sorry you had to go through this."

"Me too. It's my girls I worry the most about." Ada's voice drifted off. "I wish I could see them one last time."

"Maybe one day, Ada."

The following morning, the attendant remembered their short interaction from the previous night. She hoped they could continue the conversation but was surprised to see Ada still in bed when she entered the room. Ada usually sat gazing out the window silently praying. She put the breakfast tray down and placed her hand on Ada's neck. "You're burning up." She quickly left the room.

Ada rested in bed clutching her rosary beads. She wouldn't let them go as they dangled off the side of the bed. The attendant returned with some medicine and a cold compress to help bring the fever down. She placed the white towel on Ada's forehead and propped her up in the bed. She wasn't eating and needed to gain her strength.

"Here, drink this." The attendant attempted to place a straw at Ada's mouth but she turned away. The attendant removed the towel from Ada's forehead and tried to lift her up even farther to a sitting position. Ada was too weak, but more importantly, she wanted to be left alone to die. Determined to get her to drink, the attendant removed the straw and placed the glass to Ada's lips. Tilting it back, liquid spilled down her chin. "Come on, Ada, you have to drink." Ada turned her head again.

Barely able to talk, Ada whispered to the young lady who was trying desperately to get her to drink, "You're a kind young lady, but please, let me find heaven. It will be better for us both."

"I can't. It's my duty to care for you. Now drink this please." The worker compassionately pleaded with Ada.

Displaying a weak smile, Ada turned around to look at her. Rarely had the worker seen emotion from Ada and took the opportunity to quickly place the glass back to her lips. Ada drank a little. Her eyes sparkled with joy. The attendant was confused by the sudden change in Ada's behavior, but she continued to help her drink.

Ada envisioned her daughter helping her and took another sip. "You just reminded me of my daughter. She took care of me after my husband's beatings."

"Your husband used to beat you?" She wanted to be sure Ada wasn't delusional from the fever.

Ada turned away from the attendant and remained silent. Her smile disappeared. By her reaction, the attendant assumed she was telling the truth. She lowered Ada's head and gently placed it on the pillow. Touching Ada's shoulder to comfort her, the attendant attempted to change the topic. "You have a special little girl and a beautiful smile. Do you know that?"

Ada smiled and clutched her hand. "All these years you cared for me and I don't even know your name."

"My name is Lena."

"Lena, that's a beautiful name. Okay, let me drink some more." Lena helped her take another sip before placing the cup on the table. "Lena?"

"Yes, I'm right here. Did you need anything else?"

"Thank you for caring." She closed her eyes still daydreaming about her daughter.

Lena looked back at Ada as she walked out of the room. Thinking about what life must have been like for her, a tear rolled down her cheek. She quickly wiped it away before anyone noticed. She's not supposed to show emotion for the patients. She's not supposed to get involved.

CHAPTER 11

❧

Keeping the Faith

After hearing disappointing news from the school administrator, Pauline solemnly strolled around the neighborhood. She walked for hours thinking about what to do next and quickly learned her way around New Rochelle. She arrived home from her long walk tired and hungry. Her aunt was sitting at a table piled with dirty dishes and glasses smoking a cigarette. Pauline knew she would have to clean up after her aunt's mess, but she wanted to eat dinner first. "Aunt Bertha, is it okay if I eat now?"

"Yeah, just get me another beer first. And don't forget the bathroom needs to be done after the dishes."

Pauline dragged her tired body back to the kitchen after giving her aunt a cold beer. She quickly gobbled down the meager leftovers before tending to her nightly chores. Pauline needed to get a good night's sleep so she could start looking for work first thing in the morning.

The next morning she was desperate to start her job search. Beginning school was her top priority. It was a cold, wintry morning, but she had a plan and wasn't deterred by the inclement weather. She stepped out of the front door of the apartment building into a biting, cold wind. She wrapped her coat more tightly around her and adjusted her scarf to cover her mouth. That barely helped. The streets and sidewalks were covered with a blanket of fresh snow. The treacherous and slippery sidewalk slowed Pauline down a bit. She didn't have snow boots and her everyday shoes caused her to lose her step a few times as she walked down Main Street. It was early in the morning and only the shopkeepers were out.

Main Street was the retail hub of the city. It featured tons of stores and shopping outlets and was the "it" place to shop. Normally the streets and sidewalks were heavily congested, but it was fairly quiet as Pauline made her way to the retail shops. She suspected the overnight snow, early hour, and poor economy kept people indoors.

Pauline walked toward a store window to glance inside. She saw her reflection in the window and gasped at her ripped, dirty coat. The thin scarf covered only half of her red face. The howling wind pushed her hair back. She wondered why anyone would hire her. Pushing that thought aside, she cradled her hands around her face to peek into the store. She thought the place looked good and opened the door to enter the cigarette and candy shop. Glad to be indoors, she strolled down an aisle passing racks of candy. She paused at the counter to deliberately remove the torn scarf that covered her mouth. Her face was already windburned and her lips were chapped. An older man looked up from behind the counter. "Hello miss, pack of Camels today?" he said in a gruff voice already reaching to get the cigarettes.

"No, not today."

"Then, young lady, what brings you out on a day like this?"

"I was wondering if you have any job openings?" She grinned from ear to ear as she rubbed her hands together.

"We're lucky to still be in business at this time. Can't you see how quiet the streets are?"

Pauline didn't want to let the gentleman know she was new to the area and desperate for a job. Instead, she nodded and thanked him. She turned to walk away as she wrapped the thin scarf around her face, trying to pull it up over her mouth before going outside. "You should go home, young lady, this isn't a day to be out by yourself."

Pauline turned toward him and pulled the scarf down away from her mouth. "I don't have a choice. I have to find a job." She walked away.

Battling the vicious wind, Pauline slowly dragged herself down the snow-filled sidewalk. She paused to steady herself as a gust pushed her back. Her head was tilted down to protect her sensitive face. She stopped in front of the next store, opened the door, and entered.

The aroma of freshly baked bread overtook her senses. She didn't realize how hungry she was until she smelled the tantalizing bread.

A plump, older woman with a stained apron smiled from behind the counter. "Can I help you?"

"Hi, I would like to inquire about any job openings you might have."

"Oh my, dear, we might be closing our doors soon. We make everything fresh in the morning and if it doesn't sell, well, we lose money. With the economy these days, you are the first person to walk in today. Check back in a few months if we're still open."

Pauline bowed her head in disappointment. "Thank you anyway."

"Good luck on your search." The lady muttered under her breath. "You're gonna need it."

Pauline continued along Main Street stopping in store after store. She received the same answer from every shop owner—the economy is bad, we just laid people off, we have no customers, we're about to close down shop. However, Pauline refused to give up. She knew there had to be a job somewhere and trudged down the sidewalk in the cold, blistering wind. There weren't many people around, but Pauline was determined. Her hair looked gray from the icicles forming at the tips. She kept telling herself to keep going. She had faith that she would find a job.

The following morning, Pauline was getting ready to continue with her job search when her aunt heard her moving around the living room. Aunt Bertha walked in with a cloud of smoke circling around her head and barked, "I need more cigarettes."

"I'll be sure to get them today." Eager to leave, Pauline grabbed her scarf. It never fully dried and was still damp and stiff from the day before. She cringed as she put it around her neck.

"Make sure you pick them up, I'm almost out."

Pauline stepped outside the apartment building grateful to be outdoors. It was a beautiful, sunny morning and she had a good feeling about getting a job. The sunshine rejuvenated her spirit after being cooped up in the dingy, dark apartment with her aunt. She was glad to be away from her. Although it was still bitterly cold, the wind had died down making walking much easier. Overnight, a thin layer of freshly fallen snow blanketed the ground. She passed a few men shoveling the snow off the sidewalk. She wondered where they were the day before.

"Good morning," she said exuberantly. She could see her breath from the cold temperatures when she spoke. The men looked at her and tipped their caps. She strolled down the sidewalk.

She felt good about the day's prospects and was positive that she would find a job. Letting out a big sigh, she paused in front of a general store. She opened the door and walked toward the counter.

"What can I get you?" The man was busy organizing merchandise on the countertop and didn't look up.

Pauline was surprised by his curt demeanor but still asked, "I would like to inquire if you have any job openings?"

"Job openings?" The man lifted his head to look at her. "Ma'am, I just laid off two workers. The depression is killing my business. I'm sorry, but I have nothing."

"That's okay, thank you anyway." She coughed into her sleeve. Still very determined, she confidently walked out and continued down the street to the next shop. She was moving fairly quickly and bumped into a lady sweeping the floor as she opened the door.

The lady stumbled back and turned toward Pauline. "Good morning. It looks like you're in a rush today."

"I'm so sorry for almost knocking you over. Can I have a pack of Camels please?"

"I think I might have a few left. Let me check." The lady rested her broom against the rack and walked toward the counter.

"By the way, would you happen to have any job openings? I could do that sweeping for you." Pauline tried to entice her.

"Oh, dear, check back in a few months if—"

"You're still open." Pauline interjected.

"I guess that's what you've been hearing? Everyone's been affected terribly by the depression."

"That's okay. There has to be a job out there somewhere."

The lady placed a pack of cigarettes on top of the counter. She noticed Pauline's tattered coat as she reached into her purse for loose change. As the lady counted the money, she felt sorry for her. "It's just a suggestion but you should try one of the factories."

"What factories?"

"There are a few on the south side of town. It's hard work and they're far, but give it a try if you can't find anything around here."

"Thank you. You've been very helpful."

"Good luck, young lady. You'll surely need it."

Pauline was glad to get the suggestion since she hadn't been aware of any factories nearby. She wondered why no one had mentioned them to her before as she continued down the sidewalk. It had been a long, grueling day of disappointments, but she decided to try one more store. Pulling hard to open the door, Pauline had barely stepped inside the store when a man wiping down the counter yelled, "We're closed."

"I was just looking to see if you have any job openings," she replied from the doorway.

Laughing, the man shouted back. "Jobs? I'm sorry, I just had to let my best worker go."

"Thank you anyway." She covered her mouth to contain her cough as she turned to leave.

"You should go home now. A young lady shouldn't be walking the streets alone at night."

Deflated and tired, she headed home. She needed to clear her mind, eat, and get some rest, but as she climbed the stairs to her aunt's apartment, she heard ruckus coming from inside. She surmised her aunt was entertaining again and a long night of clean-up was ahead of her. Pauline leaned against the wall before going inside and slid down into a crouched position. She cried into her cold, wet hands.

Aunt Bertha and a few ladies sat at a table playing cards. Pauline noticed plenty of beer cans covering the table when she walked in. It was hard to see their faces through the thick smoke rings. She started coughing again and barely heard her aunt talking. "Pauline, how did it go today?" Her aunt was more curious than concerned.

"Still nothing." She had a coughing fit and was barely able to continue. "I get the same answer from everyone." Pauline walked toward the kitchen to get a glass of water.

"Did you at least get my cigarettes?"

Pauline placed the pack in front of her aunt and entered the kitchen. "Okay, my friends are hungry. We've been waiting for you. Cook us something to eat now." Aunt Bertha turned away from Pauline and dealt the next round.

Trying to keep her composure, Pauline stood completely still before responding. Tired, worn down, and without other options she was afraid to say no to her aunt. Aunt Bertha was busy playing cards and didn't notice Pauline's hesitation.

The ladies were all having a grand time and filled the room with laughter. Aunt Bertha bellowed above the loud voices. "We can use a refill. Bring us all fresh beers and clean up this mess."

"Okay, Aunt Bertha," she said as she brought several cans of beer from the kitchen.

One of the ladies, Mary, had been watching Pauline and noticed her frail state. She reached out and grabbed her arm as she placed the cans of beer on the table. "Excuse me, Pauline, you need to take care of that cough and get some rest."

"She'll be fine, she's young," Aunt Bertha interjected as she shot her friend an annoyed glance.

Ignoring her friend's stern look, Mary stood up, put her arm around Pauline and helped her to the couch. "You get some rest. I'll take care of tonight."

Aunt Bertha immediately stated, "No, she needs to earn her keep. What do you think she's here for?"

The other ladies looked down fiddling with the cards. They were afraid to look up or get involved. Furious, Mary snapped at her old friend, "You should be ashamed of yourself, Bertha. She's exhausted and sick. Can't you see that?"

"You rest now." Mary turned back toward Pauline and draped a blanket over her.

Pauline met her aunt's gaze. She knew she would have to pay for this, but she really needed to rest. She closed her eyes and drifted off to sleep.

CHAPTER 12

⚬↝⚬

Life Goes On

L ife in the orphanage didn't change for Josephine. It was the same routine every day. Although Pauline was only gone a short while, Josephine really missed her, especially at night. Every evening in the dark room, Josephine glanced at the bed next to her expecting to see her older sister. Instead, another child was fast asleep. She longed for their nighttime talks. In its place, she clutched her favorite childhood doll and often cried herself to sleep. She missed her so much already.

Although there were plenty of girls at the orphanage, Josephine felt alone for the first time in her life. Her sister had always been by her side, helping her and protecting her. Even though new girls came into the orphanage all the time, none of them were Josephine's age. She was the oldest and the longest resident. Every morning when she scrubbed the bathroom floor, she was painfully aware of how long she had been doing that chore. Sister Theresa frequently brought new girls to help her. Remembering what it was like when she was the new girl and no one talked to her, she had great empathy and spoke to them while working. Usually, their conversations went like this.

"Hopefully, one day you'll get adopted and won't have to do this for as long as I have." Josephine would start.

"Why, how long have you been here?"

"Over ten years now."

"You've been scrubbing floors for over ten years?"

"Yes, but it feels like twenty." Josephine laughed out loud every time she said it.

"How come you never got adopted?"

"I don't know. Maybe because I don't do good in school."

"I don't like it either."

Sister Theresa was usually lurking in the hallway often listening to the girls. After a short while she would break up the conversation if they were talking too long. She would stand in the doorway. "This isn't recess time, girls. Let's hurry up and finish." The girls would immediately get back to work the moment Sister Theresa appeared. Josephine was familiar with Sister Theresa's drill by now. It never changed, but it didn't deter her from talking to the new girls.

Although Josephine knew Pauline was staying with their aunt, she was worried about her. Pauline hadn't written since she left the orphanage. She desperately wanted to hear from her and know she was okay. One evening, like every other before, she looked over at the bed next to her. Overcome with concern, she whispered just like they did together for years. "I know you can hear me. I miss you. I'm worried. Please, stay safe."

And as though God answered her prayer the following day, a young girl approached Josephine and said, "Sister Sarah would like to see you. She's in the front office." Josephine couldn't imagine what the young nun wanted but immediately went to see her.

"You wanted to see me?" Josephine blurted as soon as she entered the office. The nun looked up from behind the desk and reached into her top drawer. Smiling, she handed Josephine an envelope. "What's this?"

"It just came today. It's addressed from your sister."

Quickly, Josephine ripped it open. She sat down and pulled out the note. Josephine read is quietly to herself.

Dear Josie,

I hope this letter finds you well…and you've been studying hard! It's been over six months now and I haven't been able to find a job or start nursing school yet. Aunt Bertha has me doing all the chores around the house. I think that's the only reason she agreed to take me in. That's okay because I'm still determined to be a nurse.

I miss you and love you.

Pauli

P.S. Say hi to Sister Sarah for me.

Josephine placed the letter back into the envelope and stared at it for a moment. Sister Sarah watched her, waiting to hear the news, but instead noticed tears rolling down her cheeks.

"Josephine, why are you crying? How is she doing?"

Wiping away the tears she said, "She hasn't started school yet."

"How come?"

"I don't know. She mentioned about not being able to find a job."

"Is she okay?"

"I think so, but she's doing all Aunt Bertha's chores."

Sister Sarah bowed her head in silent prayer.

Back in the institution, Ada sat up in bed alert and strong. The virus had passed. Lena walked in the room holding a tray of food. "You look much better, Ada." Lena placed the tray across the table. "So, tell me about your daughters."

Ada's eyes lit up. "I'm blessed with two great girls. I just hope they're okay. Pauline is the oldest and all she ever wanted to do was become a nurse. While the other children played outside, she preferred to stay inside and play nurse. Taking blood pressure readings was always her favorite..." Her voice trailed off.

Lena didn't want her to sink into a depression and kept the conversation upbeat. "Tell me about your other daughter."

Ada perked back up. "Josephine, my baby, all she wanted to do was play outdoors with the other kids. She hated to study or read. She's the social one. She's so young..." Ada's voice trailed off again.

Lena glanced around to make sure they were alone. She leaned in close to Ada and whispered, "I'm not allowed to get involved, but I'm going to try and find them."

"Why would you help me? I don't want you to get into trouble."

Confiding in Ada, Lena said, "I've got two girls myself. I couldn't imagine if I never saw or spoke to them again. They're my life."

"Two girls? I never knew." Ada blushed, embarrassed by her poor manners. She looked away from Lena. "I'm so sorry I never asked about you or your family. You've been so kind to me."

"After what you've been through, I would like to help you if I could."

Ada reached for her hand. "I could never repay you for that."

"If you see them, that would be enough for me. A mother-daughter bond is special." Lena thought about her own relationship with her two girls.

Ada squeezed Lena's hand affectionately. "I'm blessed with them and now I'm blessed with you."

"Where do they live?"

"I'm not sure. We lived at Colonial Villa. I don't know where they are now..." Ada's voice trailed off.

Lena firmly squeezed Ada's hand to bring her back. "Don't you worry. I'll find them." Lena walked out.

⚬

Through the years, Harry's life didn't change much. He lived in the same apartment and worked at the shoe factory warehouse. He never thought about his family or visited them. In fact, while being on his own, his drinking increased to a point where he was never sober. He drank day and night, even when at the job. The warehouse was a large open room with rows and rows of shelving and stacked boxes. It didn't have any windows and the dirty concrete floors needed a good sweeping.

Most workers hustled around moving boxes. Harry sluggishly trudged down an aisle. Overheated and tired, he stopped. Unable to stand on his own, he leaned against a stack of boxes to steady himself. The floor manager saw him from the distance and walked over to him. "Another break, Harry? What's the matter this time?" The manager stood with his arms crossed across his chest glaring at him.

"I don't feel right today. I'm burning up in here." Harry wiped the sweat off his forehead with his dirty hand.

The supervisor noticed his red face but had little sympathy for him. "Well, maybe you should lay off the booze for once. You never feel right."

"That's none of your concern." Harry was agitated that he wasn't shown any compassion.

"It's my concern when every time I look at you, you're leaning against a box. Now let's go, back to work!"

Furious, Harry glared at the manager as he stood up and balanced himself. He trudged to the open floor where the men were busy moving boxes. The manager, tired of his games, turned to check on Harry as he yelled across the floor, "Keep this up and you'll be looking for a new job."

Later that evening after tucking her children into bed, Lena was determined to find Harry. Thrilled to get the lead from Ada, she hustled up two flights of stairs in the Rolfe building. She looked down at her handwritten note to confirm the address. Standing in front of Harry's apartment door, Lena paused a moment before knocking. Ada had warned her about Harry's temper and she wanted to be sure she had her wits about her. She knocked. No one answered. She banged harder on the door. Still no one answered. She waited a while longer expecting that he would be home due to the late hour. Disappointed, she left.

CHAPTER 13

＠◯

Perseverance Wins Out

It was July, approximately seven months after Pauline left the orphanage. Although the weather changed to hazy, hot, and humid, her spirit remained unaffected. She was still as determined as ever to find a job. Like every other morning, she placed a fresh, folded towel over the shower rail and wiped the sink clean before heading out. "Aunt Bertha, I'm leaving. I'm going to try one of the factories today."

"Go ahead, but they'll never hire you. You don't have any experience working in a factory." Her aunt tried to dissuade her.

"I'm running out of options, though. I tried every store around here. Some a few times."

"Don't forget, I need you home later. The ladies are coming over again." Aunt Bertha handed Pauline a grocery list. "And pick these up. Don't be late."

Pauline took the list from her aunt. "How could you afford to gamble all the time?"

"It's not gambling." Aunt Bertha threw her head back roaring in laughter. "It's how I make my living."

"By taking all your friends' money?" Pauline was flabbergasted.

"They're fine. Their husbands are still around. I need to worry about myself right now."

Pauline shrugged her aunt off and walked outside into the hot, summer morning. She had a mission and strode down Main Street. Already hot and flushed from the heat, she was grateful for her loose clothing. She had a long walk ahead of her, but didn't mind being outside the apartment. She was relieved to be away from her aunt. A slight breeze filled the air. She thought that even a hot breeze was better than no breeze. She walked miles to get to the commercial zone. She was in the general area but unsure exactly where the factories were located. She turned down a desolate street. There were a few big, old brick buildings. She didn't see any company signs, but luckily she saw a police officer down the road. She approached him and said, "Excuse me, sir, can you tell me where the nearest factory is?"

"Which one? This place is loaded with factories." The officer smirked.

"Really? How about the closest one."

"Right there." He pointed to a door across from where they were standing.

"Oh, thank you, sir." Pauline shrugged and headed toward the door. She entered the large room. It was noisy from the tapping of sewing machines running in the background. The sound reverberated through the open room and drowned out all other noise.

She quickly surveyed the room and counted five machines per table with a woman operating each machine. There were rows and rows of tables going down the length of the room. She guessed around one hundred workers sat on hard, wooden chairs working diligently. The ceilings were very high and lights hung low from long poles tethered to the ceiling. No one looked up or noticed a stranger in the room. Not sure of where to go, Pauline stood still and looked around. She had never seen so many machines going all at once. A lady approached her, but Pauline couldn't hear her coming. The woman touched Pauline's arm to get her attention. "Excuse me, miss, can I help you?"

"Oh, I'm terribly sorry. I couldn't hear you with all this noise."

"Yes, it's very loud in here. You get used to it after a while. It's hot in the summer and cold in the winter. That, I never get used to. Anyway, I'm the manager, what can I do for you?"

"I'm looking for a job. Do you have any openings?"

The manager stared at Pauline without uttering a word, but took a moment to look her up and down. Pauline was self-conscious from traveling in the heat, plus the factory air inside was hotter than outside. Pauline watched the expression on the manager's face, she had seen the same look many times already. Pauline glanced down bracing herself for disappointment. However, the long pause was too much for Pauline to take. She assumed by her silence that there were no positions open. Pauline didn't wait for her to answer and said, "I know, not right now, the economy is tight." She dabbed her forehead with a handkerchief and walked away.

"Why are you leaving so quickly?" the manager yelled out to her.

Pauline stopped to answer her. "I've been looking for months for a job and have heard the same thing over and over."

"Why would an attractive young lady like you want to work here?"

Pauline walked back toward her. "My dream is to go to nursing school, but I can't afford it without a job."

"Your parents can't afford it either?"

"I don't know where my parents are. I grew up in an orphanage. I was dropped off when I was eight."

The manager fell silent again. She was intrigued with Pauline's story and decided to offer her a chance. "Okay. I give you credit. I do have one opening, but it's a late shift."

Pauline couldn't believe what she heard. She immediately snapped it up before it was taken away from her. "I don't care, I'll take it!"

"I don't usually hire young ladies like you, but I admire your determination."

Unable to contain her enthusiasm, Pauline blurted out, "When can I start?"

"Next Monday. And dress in light clothes. It still gets very hot at night." The manager cautioned.

"What time?"

"You'll start with the four to eleven shift. We'll see how it goes."

"I'll be here. Thank you so much." Pauline couldn't contain her happiness and uncharacteristically hugged her before walking away.

Pauline practically skipped all the way to the nursing school from the factory. She couldn't wait to tell Sister Margaret that she had found a job and could start school. After being rejected for months, her determination had finally paid off.

When Pauline arrived at the school, she raced down the hall to the admissions office. She opened the door and darted toward Sister Margaret with a beaming smile. Hearing the ruckus, Sister Margaret looked up from her desk and was surprised to see Pauline standing there with a huge grin.

"Pauline, I was concerned about you. Where have you been?" Sister Margaret calmly asked.

Pauline caught her breath. "I've been having a difficult time finding a job, but finally I found one. I can start school now."

"That's great news. Where are you working?" The nun smiled, genuinely pleased for her.

"At a girdle factory from four to eleven." Pauline had a hard time containing her happiness until she saw the nun's smile erase from her face.

"My, dear, how do you plan on going to school all day and then work until eleven?" Sister Margaret knew the demands of the program.

"I'll find a way to do it. I can, I promise." Pauline was nervous the nun would retract her application.

"What about your homework? When will you find time for that?"

"I'll stay up all night if I have to. When can I start?"

The nun knew it would be difficult for her to keep up with her studies. But she also never saw another student with as much drive and determination as the woman standing before her. She couldn't let her down. "I can place you in the fall semester. You'll be taking the majority of your classes at the hospital around the corner."

Pauline was ecstatic. "I can't wait to tell my sister. Thank you so much, Sister Margaret. This is the happiest day of my life."

Gliding down the hallway, Pauline's thoughts turned to her mother. Smiling, she whispered, "Mom I'm doing it. I'm going to be a nurse."

Walking home from the admissions office, Pauline's feet barely touched the ground. As she approached the door to her aunt's apartment, she could hear the ladies howling inside. She was determined to not let anything ruin her day. She grabbed hold of the doorknob and sprung through the front door. As usual, the ladies were having a grand time and the table was covered with beer cans and ash trays filled with cigarette butts. She quickly walked passed them to place the groceries in the kitchen. While putting them away, she was bursting with happiness and couldn't hold in her news any longer. She exclaimed, "I did it, Aunt Bertha! I'm starting nursing school in September."

"You found a job?" Aunt Bertha was shocked.

"Yes, at a girdle factory." Pauline walked quickly toward the bathroom and closed the door behind her. She didn't want her aunt's direct comments to dampen her spirit. Even so, she was curious about what she might say to the other ladies and kept the door slightly ajar.

Aunt Bertha looked down and didn't say a word. Mary was truly happy for Pauline and was the first to speak. "That's great news. I'm happy for her, Bertha."

"She'll never survive doing my chores, going to school, and working. Never."

"Bertha, she's a very determined young lady. You should be proud of her. Lay off her a bit."

Aunt Bertha snapped at her friend, "It'll be too much for her, believe me. I'll see to it." She directed her unhappiness toward Mary. Unfazed by the outburst, Mary didn't reply. They had been friends a long time and she knew Bertha meant business.

Pauline was secretly listening when her aunt called out to her. "Pauline, we need something to eat and more drinks. What's taking you so long in there? Get out here!"

"Okay, Aunt Bertha, in a minute." Pauline's suspicions were confirmed. Her aunt took her in for selfish reasons.

CHAPTER 14

✦

Getting Closer

Outside in the backyard of the orphanage, Josephine swayed alone on a swing until she was summoned to Sister Sarah's office by another girl. Josephine entered the front office. "Hello, Sister Sarah, you wanted to see me?"

"Take this and read it. It's great news." Sister Sarah handed her an opened envelope. Josephine grinned and her eyes lit up as she pulled out the letter to read.

Dear Sister Sarah,

I finally found a job and can't tell you how excited I am to start nursing school. My dream is finally coming true. Please let Josie know I'm doing well and that I love her. I couldn't have done this without your help. I'll write again soon with all the details.

Love, Pauline

When she finished reading, Josephine looked up as tears glistened in her eyes. "She did it. She's finally going to nursing school." Wiping the tears away she said, "I'm so proud of her. My sister is really remarkable."

"You're both unique and remarkable in your own ways. Never forget that when you start your own journey." Josephine looked away from the nun. She didn't believe she was remarkable, at least not like her sister.

More determined than ever to find Harry, Lena went back to Colonial Villa apartments. Once again, she climbed two flights of stairs and paused in front of Harry's apartment door. After steadying herself for what might come next, she knocked. No one answered. She wondered if he was ever home. She banged on the door loudly but didn't expect him to answer. She decided it was time to find another way.

The following morning, Lena didn't want to deliver the bad news to Ada since she was finally starting to show progress. However, Lena needed her help with another lead and was thinking about what to do next when she entered Ada's stark room. It took her a second to notice the chair and bed were empty. After looking in the bathroom, she realized Ada wasn't there. She frantically ran down the hallway to the common room area. Glancing around, she spotted Ada sitting silently in a chair saying her rosary.

Lena calmly walked up to her. "There you are, Ada. What made you decide to join the others?"

Ada looked around the room as if she was seeing it for the first time. It was plain with simple table and chair sets. She noticed that all the patients were dressed in white gowns. Many of them just sat and gazed into space without uttering a word. Others aimlessly wandered around with a purpose, but no direction. A few patients walked up to her and stared, fixated by her presence since they had never seen her before. Ada looked down at herself and noticed the white gown she was wearing. She realized that she was dressed just like them and held her rosary beads tighter.

Ada looked up at Lena and said, "I'm hopeful that I might get a chance to see my daughters again. There is nothing more I want." She smiled. "It's because of you."

Lena was pleased with Ada's progress. She made a positive step forward and was finally coming around. However, deep inside, she knew that she wasn't any closer to finding the girls.

"I'm trying the best I can for you. I'll keep at it."

"I know you are. You'll find them. I know you will."

Lena couldn't break her spirit and update her on the news. Not yet at least.

That evening, Lena walked into Ada's room with the dinner tray. Now that she was back in her own space, Lena decided to tell her she had hit a dead end. She started slowly and said, "I'm so happy to see that you finally joined the others."

"Me too, but honestly, no one talked to me so I might as well just stay here."

"No, it's good to get out of this room. You should go every day." Lena peeked around to make sure no one else was listening. She leaned in to get closer to Ada and whispered, "I went to the apartment twice already. No one was there."

Ada's eyes glazed over. She reached for her locket and rubbed it between her fingers. "Maybe he moved."

"I can try his job. Where does he work?"

"At the shoe factory in Lodi. He works in the warehouse."

Lena touched her hand, nodded, and walked out. She was glad to have a new lead.

The next morning before work, Lena went to the shoe factory determined to find Harry. She walked around the large building to the loading dock to avoid getting stopped by the office workers. Upon entering the warehouse, she paused for a moment amazed at how high the boxes were stacked.

"Can I help you, ma'am?"

The sound of a man's voice startled her and she stammered a reply. "Hi, I'm looking for Mr. Roka."

"He got hurt and has been out. Try back in a few weeks."

"Okay, thank you. I will."

KEEPING IT ALL TOGETHER
1937

⤬

CHAPTER 15

School's In Session

It was a cool, September evening in 1937. Pauline had been working steadily now for a few months. The factory air was stale and the racket from the sewing machines echoed throughout the large room. It was a steady, nerve-racking sound. Even though it was cool outside, Pauline sat at the sewing machine trying to keep the sweat from dripping onto the fabric. She wiped it from her forehead and then wrapped her scarf around her head. It did the trick. The work was easy but tedious. She placed the cloth on the table and carefully guided it as the needle penetrated through the fabric. At first, the vibration from the machine made it difficult to guide the material in a straight line. Now an expert, she quickly moved through her stack of cloth. She worked mechanically, but her mind drifted to the promise of the next day. It was her first day of school. She was nervous and excited at the same time. And couldn't wait for her shift to be over.

Once she stepped into the night's crisp air, she rushed home, practically sprinting the whole way. She wanted to get everything together and settled for school before going to sleep. Of course, she had a full list of chores to do first. After rushing to complete most of her tasks, she was finally able to collapse onto the couch. However, she tossed and turned all night long unable to sleep in anticipation of her first day. When morning broke, she rolled off of the couch and entered the kitchen. Her aunt sat at the table waiting for her to wake up. She had a lot on her mind and was eager to unload it on her niece. Surprised to see her sitting there, Pauline said, "Oh, I didn't realize you're up already."

Without hesitating, Aunt Bertha quickly snapped, "You didn't finish the dishes last night."

Pauline glanced toward the sink and saw a few unwashed dishes. "It was late when I got home. I did all the other chores but didn't want to wake you running the water."

"Never mind that, you make sure your chores are completed every day before you go to sleep. Am I clear?"

"Yes, Aunt Bertha."

"When is your first day of school?"

"Today. I'm so excited!" She was not going to let her aunt ruin her day. She had been waiting for this her whole life and wasn't going to let anything or anyone jeopardize it.

"Well, considering it's going to be a long day for you, make sure the apartment is swept before you leave and clean the dishes." Aunt Bertha sneered as she walked away.

Pauline quickly got ready and tended to her morning chores before heading to school.

Arriving at the hospital, she paused to read the large sign on the building, Intention Hospital. She giggled in excitement before entering as she realized that her dream was finally coming true.

Bursting through the doorway of the building, Pauline was immediately overwhelmed by the number of students talking and hustling to class. In all the frenzy, she was having trouble finding her first class and was frantically wandering through the hallways. Overcome by the number of adjoining halls and classrooms, she was trying to read the number over a door and accidentally bumped into another student. Both of their books crashed down on the ground. Mortified, Pauline immediately bent down to pick up the books. When she stood up, she faced a thin, pretty lady with a short, trendy hairstyle. Fascinated by the number of waves she had in her hair, Pauline took a second before handing her the books. "I'm so sorry," she said.

"It's okay. Are you lost?"

"Well, um, yes. It's my first day here. I have no idea where I'm going." Pauline admitted hoping to get some help.

"What room are you heading to?"

Flustered by their collision, Pauline couldn't remember and looked at her schedule. "Room 102 in the Hamilton Hallway."

"You can come with me, I'm headed that way. Didn't you go to the spring orientation?"

"No, I wasn't officially enrolled then."

"Oh, that explains it." They both walked down the hallway together. "So, what's your name?"

"Pauline."

"What a pretty name. I'm Dolores, my friends call me Dolly. It's also my first day and my parents are so frightened I'm here alone. I'm sure yours are too."

Pauline didn't reply and looked down. Dolly picked up on her silence. "I'm sorry, did I say something wrong?"

"No, it's just that I haven't seen my parents since I was a young girl."

"Really? Why?"

"My sister and I were dropped off at an orphanage."

"Wow, how old were you?"

"Eight."

"Gee. I'm so sorry."

"It's okay. I'm used to it by now. You had no way of knowing."

Dolly paused by a door. "This is it, Biology 101."

After class, Pauline found her way to the cafeteria. She was hungry and needed some time to regroup. So far Biology 101 was more confusing and harder than she expected. She sat by herself with her tray of food. This was her first time in the cafeteria and she was observing everyone around her. Many students were laughing and enjoying themselves, others were deep in conversation, and a few sat alone and studied while they ate. Soon Pauline became preoccupied with her own thoughts.

"How's your first day going so far?" Startled, Pauline nearly jumped out of her seat. When she looked up, Dolly was standing at the table.

Welcoming the company Pauline said, "The classes are harder than I thought."

Dolly laughed. "I feel the same way. Can I sit?"

"Please."

Dolly sat across from Pauline and noticed her friend Millie quickly approaching with a lunch tray. Millie, without regard to anyone else, barreled into the seat and immediately interjected, "Dolly, I've been looking for you all morning."

Dolly ignored her comment and introduced her. "Millie, this is Pauline."

Millie nodded.

Pauline smiled. "Hello, Millie, nice to meet you." Millie didn't hear a word that Pauline said. Her eyes were fixated on a young, handsome man who just entered the room. She watched him intently. Pauline followed her gaze. Impeccably groomed, his dark hair was neatly parted on one side. He casually strolled through the room with his hands in his pockets nodding to people and greeting them along the way.

"Hello ladies," he said grinning as he walked passed their table.

"Hello, Walter." Millie gazed, studying him as he walked down the aisle. Millie turned toward Dolly. "Hopefully one day I'll get to date him. He's so gorgeous."

Dolly shot her a look. "Keep on dreaming, Millie. Everyone wants to date him." Curious, Pauline craned her neck to see around Dolly just as he turned back around. Their eyes met. Walter nodded and gave her a friendly smile. Heat rushed into Pauline's face and she quickly turned away. She had never interacted with a man before.

Millie noticed their pleasant exchange. She was not pleased.

Later that afternoon, Pauline was glad to have the jitters of the first day of school behind her. She hurried down the sidewalk. She needed to get moving if she was to make it to the factory on time.

"Pauline!"

Hearing her name called, she kept walking but turned around and noticed Dolly racing toward her.

"I'm not sure if you're interested but some of the girls are having a get together at the boarding house later. Why don't you come?" Dolly offered an invitation.

"I can't. I have to work from four to eleven. Thank you anyway."

"You work too?"

"It's the only way I'm able to go to school. I have to run so I'm not late. See you tomorrow."

Dolly smiled and waved goodbye as Pauline raced away.

Already exhausted from the day, Pauline's adrenaline started to wear off and she still had seven hours of work to go. At the end of her shift, she dragged herself across the room and headed toward the door. The manager stopped her before she left and said, "You're doing a fantastic job, Pauline."

Pauline nodded. "Thank you."

"Do you feel okay?"

"Just tired, but I'll be fine. See you tomorrow afternoon." She turned to walk out into the dark night. The street was eerily quiet and desolate. Suddenly, Pauline felt alone and frightened. She quickened her pace, but her body dragged behind her. "I miss you mom," she said looking up to the stars. "Please watch over me during my travels."

Pauline kept up the exhaustive pace for five months. She was thin and pale; her sparkle dimmed. It was the dead of winter now and the streets were covered with snow. Her trek to and from work in the bitter cold was wearing on her. The wind bit right through her and she was constantly chilled to the bone. No matter how hard she tried, she couldn't get warm.

Stepping out of the hospital, the continuous flapping of the flag grated on her nerves. She was always on edge now. The wind howled loudly and she barely heard Dolly calling out to her.

"Do you have to go to work tonight in this weather?"

"Yes, I have to. They never shut the factory down and I can't miss work or they'll replace me. I have to pay the tuition next month."

"You need a break, Pauline, you can't keep this pace up." Dolly was genuinely concerned. She saw the toll the grueling schedule was taking on her.

"Unfortunately, I don't have any other options," she said as she coughed into her sleeve.

"You sound terrible. You need to go home and rest, not work."

Standing next to Dolly, Millie listened to the exchange and couldn't remain quiet any longer. She blurted out, "What are you, her mother?"

Dolly glared at Millie for being so insensitive. Touching Pauline's arm before she spoke she said, "I know I keep asking you to come to the boarding house party, try to make it this Saturday."

"I'll see, Dolly. I really have to run. See you tomorrow."

Pauline walked away and as soon as she was out of earshot, Millie spat at Dolly, "Why are you so concerned with her?"

Dolly shrugged her shoulders. "I don't know. There's something about her. She's different from us."

Millie's distaste for Pauline was evident. "Yeah, she's just a poor girl from an orphanage. That's it."

"No, it's her drive and determination that impresses me. Look what she's doing just to be a nurse."

Millie snapped, "It doesn't matter. She'll never finish school anyway."

Dolly watched Pauline trample through the snow filled sidewalk and stated, "I think she will."

Later that evening nearing the end of her shift, Pauline slouched over the sewing machine. Her head was heavy from exhaustion and she was barely able to hold it up. The warehouse's high ceiling trapped the heat above the work area making it bitterly cold in the wintertime. Pauline wore layers of heavy clothing to stay warm but needed to keep her fingers exposed to thread the fabric. By the end of her shift, her fingertips were frozen stiff. She frequently paused to blow into her hands to add some warmth to them. Steam formed around her mouth from breathing heavy. It was all becoming too much. Her body started to succumb to her exhaustion. She just wanted to lie down and go to sleep. Her eyes started to close, her head tilted lower as the manager approached her from behind.

"Pauline, you've been falling behind, that's not like you."

Pauline jolted awake and quickly grabbed another piece of cloth. "I'm sorry. I've just been a little worn out lately."

"I'm sorry to tell you this, but if you can't keep up I'll have to replace you."

Pauline quickly sat up straight. Her eyes opened wide. "No, please, I really need this job. I'll catch up. I'll do whatever it takes."

"I would hate to have to let you go. Please don't make me."

"I won't, I promise." Her heart thumped violently against her chest as she slid the fabric across the machine. Adrenaline jolted her awake and eased her frozen fingers.

Glad when the shift was finally over, Pauline headed outdoors to walk home. Her thoughts drifted to easier times when she was in the orphanage. She didn't know how she was going to make it through the next year and a half. She hoped there was another way. Upon entering the apartment, she was surprised to see her aunt playing cards with the ladies. She was totally worn out and barely able to remove her jacket. Her aunt watched her struggle. There was a smirk of satisfaction on her face as she called out to her, "Don't forget the bathroom needs to be done tonight."

Pauline nodded without saying a word. She was too tired for interaction. Mary shook her head with dissatisfaction but didn't say a word.

Later that evening, Pauline's head hit the pillow like a ton of bricks. Even though she didn't stir all night, she wasn't able to sleep long enough to rejuvenate her overtired body. She was running on empty and sitting in class the next day, she struggled to stay awake. Her head nodded down and eyelids slowly closed as the teacher noticed she was starting to fall asleep. "Excuse me, Miss Roka, are we keeping you awake today?"

Pauline's head quickly lifted up, but she remained in a daze for the rest of the class. She was unable to focus on the teacher's lesson. Dolly observed her friend's stupor from across the classroom. She felt horrible for her and quickly went to her at recess. As they walked down the hallway together to the cafeteria Dolly said, "It's none of my business, but you're not going to last this way."

They both sat at an empty table to eat their lunch. Pauline rested her elbow on the table and plopped her head in her hand. She had lost her fire. "I told you, Dolly, I don't have a choice. I have to work if I want to be a nurse." She let out a big sigh. "I don't have any other options."

Deep in conversation, neither girl noticed Walter walking toward them with his lunch tray. "Would either of you mind if I join you?" Full of energy, he was unaware of the serious discussion they were engaged in.

Dolly quickly responded, "Of course not, doctor."

Pauline perked up immediately. Trying to hold her head up high she added, "Sure."

Walter smiled and took a seat next to Pauline flashing his perfectly straight and white teeth. Pauline noticed that he was always impeccably groomed. She smoothed her hair down, self-conscious about how she looked.

"I haven't seen you around for a while, doctor. Where have you been?" Dolly said curiously.

"Please, call me Walter. I volunteer at the Mt. Vernon Infirmary doing hands-on training for young doctors starting their residency. I enjoy helping out when they need me. I'm glad to be back though." He looked at Pauline. Dolly noticed his glance and wanted to give them some time alone so she excused herself to use the ladies room. As a true gentleman, a result of good breeding, Walter stood as Dolly got up from the table to walk away.

Pauline shot Dolly a piercing stare. She had never been alone with a man before. She didn't know what to say. Walter sensed her shyness and started the conversation. "So, tell me about yourself, Pauline."

"How do you know my name?"

Walter raised his eyebrows and pointed at her books. Across the top in neat penmanship displayed the name, Pauline Roka.

"Oh, I guess that was easy."

Walter grinned and egged her on. "Soooo?"

Pauline didn't know what to say. She didn't want to tell him the truth. "There's not much to know. Believe me." She shrugged.

"Okay. I'll go first. I lived in Bronxville my whole life and went to high school there. I finished medical school in Pennsylvania. Okay, your turn."

Pauline hesitated and looked away from him for a second. She returned her gaze and without pausing decided to tell him the truth. "I lived in an orphanage since I was eight with my sister. I don't know if my parents are currently alive and I work in a girdle factory so I can attend school."

Walter howled. "Come on, seriously."

Pauline looked down, her face flushed. "It's the truth."

He looked at her, softening his voice he said, "I'm really sorry. I thought you were only kidding."

"It's okay. Most people don't believe me anyway."

"Are you living at the boarding house with Dolly?"

"No, at my aunt's apartment about twenty blocks away."

"You walk back and forth everyday?" Walter was overtaken with her situation.

"Yes, I walk everywhere. The only thing that bothers me is walking alone after I get out of work at eleven o'clock."

"You walk the streets by yourself at night?" He was flabbergasted. Pauline nodded. She didn't want to talk about it any longer and was glad when Dolly sat back down.

"So, did you two get acquainted?"

Pauline shook her head yes. Walter was intrigued and couldn't keep his eyes off of her. He didn't mean to embarrass her or make her feel uncomfortable. He thought about her troubled life and the burden she still carried.

Millie spotted Walter from across the room and quickly made a beeline to his table. She was surprised to see Dolly and Pauline sitting with him.

"Hi, doctor, where have you been?" Millie asked grinning from ear to ear.

Walter was still thinking about his conversation with Pauline and was oblivious to Millie's question. His eyes never left Pauline. "Hi, Millie," he said aloofly.

Millie noticed that his gaze never left Pauline. She couldn't understand what he saw in her. Dolly watched Millie's smile vanish as she plopped down on the nearest chair. She felt badly for her old friend but didn't say a word.

CHAPTER 16

A Turn of Events

Harry returned to work after having a few weeks off to rest his hurt back. He spent his time off drinking. Now, he couldn't stop. Walking through the warehouse, he rummaged through the boxes to find the whiskey bottle he hid. He took a swig and felt the warmth immediately run through his body. He took another one before stashing the bottle away. Feeling the quick effect of the alcohol, he stumbled unsteadily through the aisle. Gasping for air, he began violently coughing into his sleeve. Looking down at his blood stained shirt, he lost his balance and crashed into a large pile of boxes. The boxes gave way and tumbled on top of him as he fell to the ground.

Hearing the ruckus, the manager raced over. "What the hell is going on here?"

Harry emerged from under the boxes struggling to stand up. "I lost my balance."

Irate, the manager leaned in very close to Harry's face to smell his breath. He screamed, "You didn't lose your balance, you're drunk again. You're done. Grab your stuff and get out!"

Harry was furious. Trying to stand and gain his balance he shouted, "You can't do this! You're firing me after all these years?"

"I should have done it a long time ago. You're no good." The enraged manager walked away from him.

"You'll regret this." Harry threw his fists in the air toward the manager, almost knocking himself over.

Without turning around, the manager waved him off.

A few weeks later, the warehouse manager was busy training a new worker when Lena rushed in.

"Hi, sir, I'm looking for—"

"He no longer works here." He remembered her and immediately cut her off. He was behind schedule and had no time for anything to do with Harry. Glancing up at Lena, he noticed her shocked expression and softened a reply, "He's no good anyway. You should stay away from him."

The manager hurried away. Lena sprinted after him determined to get more information.

"Sir, I need to find him. It's for his family." The manager turned around to face her.

"Family? That no good man walked away from his family years ago."

"Please, sir, can you help me?"

The manager fell for her desperate plea. "Try the pub on the corner. That seems to be his home away from home."

"Thank you." She smiled and was glad for the information.

The pub was only a short walk from the warehouse. It was a small shack with only a few tiny windows. It desperately needed a fresh coat of paint. A faded, barely legible sign, William's Pub, hung crooked above the front door. Determined, she pulled hard on the heavy door to open it and stepped into the dingy bar, waiting a few seconds for her eyesight to adjust to the darkness. The tiny windows barely let in natural light. She canvassed the small room quickly and noticed a few men hunched over sitting at the bar. Spotting a barmaid, she approached her and said, "Excuse me, would you happen to know who Mr. Roka is?"

A disheveled looking man turned on his bar stool and in a gruff voice said, "Who's asking?"

Lena turned to look at the man. "Are you Mr. Roka?"

Demanding an answer, he responded, "Yeah, that's me. Why are you asking?"

Catching her voice she replied, "Sir, I care for your wife. Would you be kind enough to tell me where your daughters are?"

"I don't have a wife or daughters." He turned back around and downed another shot. Slamming the empty glass against the top of the bar, he slowly spun around again to face her. "Now scram, take a walk. It's been a bad week."

Lena froze. Unsure of how to proceed next, she stared at him for a moment.

"I told you to take a walk, didn't I?" Harry ran his hand through his hair and banged the side of his fist against the bar.

She wasn't ready to give up, Lena pressed on. "You don't understand..." She abruptly stopped talking the moment she saw Harry push himself up with both hands to stand up straight.

"Get lost I said. Now!"

Seeing the fury in his eyes, Lena scurried away. Ada warned her of Harry's short temper. Lena didn't want to push him too far so she forced open the door and stormed out.

The barmaid watched their exchange and placed another shot in front of Harry's stool. As soon as Harry sat back down, she rushed out the door after Lena.

"Wait!" The barmaid called out to her. Lena stopped as the woman ran toward her.

"I heard him mention to a friend one night that the girls are at an orphanage."

"Do you know where?"

"Lodi Orphanage." The barmaid looked back to make sure no one left the bar and saw them talking.

Lena hugged the barmaid. "Thank you so much, this means the world to me."

Lena couldn't wait to share the news with Ada. She was glad they were out of their father's care, especially after meeting him.

Lena rushed into the hospital the following day. She looked for Ada in her room, but she wasn't there. Lena entered the community area and quickly scanned the room, pleased to see Ada sitting among the other patients. It was a good sign, even though she still kept to herself mumbling the rosary. Lena approached her with a huge grin and got real close to Ada to whisper her news, "I think I know where they are."

Ada's eyes widened and lit up. "Are they okay?"

"They've been in an orphanage all these years."

Ada made the sign of the cross. Relieved to know her girls have been taken care of, she started to cry. Wiping her tears she said, "It's probably the best thing that could have happened to them. They're away from him."

"I'll try and go to them soon."

Ada grabbed Lena's hand. "I can't thank you enough. You are truly a blessing to me."

"Don't worry. You'll get to see them. I promise."

CHAPTER 17

A Blossoming Romance

It was a cold winter night and Pauline dreaded walking home after work. It was a long, dark trek and the streets were desolate. She dragged herself through the snowy sidewalk cautiously watching her footing so she wouldn't slip. A derelict watched her gingerly walk from across the street and called out, "Hey lady, you got spare change?"

Pauline didn't respond. She kept her eyes forward and quickened her step, but the slippery sidewalk restricted her movement. She was afraid she was going to fall.

"Come on, lady." The derelict started to move toward her.

"Please, leave me alone. I don't have any money," she said still without looking at him, but sensing he was moving closer.

He quickened his pace toward her when suddenly a car pulled out from nowhere and stopped abruptly.

"Get in," the driver said to Pauline.

Pauline started to run but slipped and fell. Walter raced out of the driver's seat. She looked up and sighed in relief when she recognized his familiar face. Walter helped her into the car and quickly drove away.

"You shouldn't be out here alone. It's not safe."

Diverting the topic, Pauline said, "Thank you for stopping. What are you doing around here this late at night?" Walter remained silent and focused on driving. He was caught off guard and didn't want to answer. Uncomfortable by his silence, Pauline pressed further. "Have you been following me?" Walter still didn't answer. "Walter, have you?" He knew he couldn't remain silent forever, she was pressing too hard.

"Yes... when you told me you walk home alone, I wanted to make sure you were okay."

"Why? Why are you doing this?"

Walter fell silent again.

"Tell me, please."

"Okay, because I care for you." Walter confessed, but his gaze never left the road. "You're not like any other girl I've ever met before."

"Why, because of all my misfortunes?"

"No," he said tenderly and glanced at her. "It's because of your drive and determination. It's inspiring to me. I've had everything easily handed to me."

"It's what I have to do to become a nurse."

"That's exactly what I mean. Despite everything you've been through, you still find the ambition to follow your dream and keep fighting for it."

"You just feel sorry for me." She lowered her voice.

"No, I don't. I find you remarkable."

"You can have any woman you want. All the ladies are after you."

"But they don't have your heart. That's what matters to me the most. I don't want any other lady."

Walter parked the car in front of Aunt Bertha's building.

"How did you know this is where I live?" Pauline asked innocently. When Walter didn't answer, she caught on. "That's right, you've been following me."

Walter reached out to hold her hand. She froze. A man had never touched her before.

"I really want to take you out to dinner. Just the two of us."

She pulled her hand away and looked down. She didn't know how to act or what to say.

Walter suspected she had never dated before. A lot had happened in one evening and he reckoned he had to go slowly. "I'm sorry for putting you on the spot like this. How about you think it over?"

"Okay, I'll think about it. Thank you for helping me tonight and for the ride." Pauline opened the door and got out. "See you tomorrow," she said waving goodbye.

Walter waved back before driving away. He hoped he didn't scare her off.

Pauline stood in the darkness and watched the car travel down the road until it was out of sight. Thinking about all that happened that evening, she didn't notice Aunt Bertha watching from the window.

Walking up the steps, she was surprised to see her aunt standing in the doorway to greet her. Pauline's huge smile immediately diminished when her aunt started peppering her with questions. "Whose car is that?"

"A doctor from the hospital."

"I thought you were working? You have no time for socializing or any of that nonsense. You're busy enough." Aunt Bertha wanted to put an immediate end to that relationship.

"He was just kind enough to give me a ride home since it's so late."

"Never mind him, you still have your chores to finish for tonight."

Pauline nodded.

❦

The following day, Pauline and Dolly were eating lunch together in the cafeteria. Pauline confided to Dolly what happened the night before. "I can't believe it. You have to go out with him!" Dolly was thrilled for her friend and tried to egg her on.

"My aunt's not crazy about it."

"Pauline, he's a good looking doctor. He's the most eligible bachelor around for pete's sake. Do you realize the opportunity you have? You have to think about yourself for once."

Millie overheard them talking as she sat next to the girls. "What opportunity?" She wanted to catch up on the conversation.

"Millie, you'll never believe it." Dolly thought it would be best for her to break the news. "Walter wants to take Pauline out to dinner."

Millie couldn't contain her disappointment. She had been after him for a long time. She looked right at Pauline and jealously shouted, "You have no business going out with him!"

Dolly immediately jumped in and responded, "How could you say that, Millie? She's our friend."

"Well, for one thing," Millie said, "she has nothing to offer him like we do."

Pauline lowered her gaze. She always suspected how Millie felt, but hearing it directly from her stung. Dolly couldn't help but notice.

"That's not right, Millie. We're friends and friends don't act that way toward each other."

"Friends don't steal each other's man either." Millie defiantly shot back.

"I'm sorry. I didn't know you two were together. I would never get in the middle." Pauline finally spoke up.

Swallowing her pride, Millie said, "Well, we're not exactly together, but I like him."

"Well, Millie, it seems he likes Pauline." Dolly was quick to defend Pauline.

Upset by the news and onslaught from Dolly, Millie stood up and stormed away.

Dolly clarified Walter and Millie's relationship. "They grew up in the same town, Bronxville. She's been chasing him for years, but he's not interested in her that way. If he was, he would've asked her out already."

"I don't want to get in the middle."

"There is no middle. You're a fool if you don't go."

Pauline didn't want to cause any trouble with Millie. She was thinking about what Dolly said while walking down the hallway to her next class. Walter spotted her from the other end of the hall and snuck up beside her. They walked a few steps together before Pauline even noticed he was there.

"Oh hello, Walter."

"You seem preoccupied. I hope you're not thinking about last night? I'm really sorry if I came on too strong."

Pauline was overtaken by his sincerity. "Okay, I'll go."

"You'll go where?" He teased, but wanted to be certain he understood her clearly.

"Out to dinner with you, if you still want to?" Her face flushed.

Flashing a huge grin he said, "Really? You will? That's great. When is your next night off?"

"Saturday."

"Saturday it is. I'll pick you up at seven."

After Pauline completed her chores on Saturday morning, she strolled into town. She had saved up a little money and wanted to buy something new to wear to dinner with Walter. She was surprised that she was actually looking forward to the evening. She hummed along the avenue peeking into different store windows. She didn't have much money, but hoped she could still find something suitable.

Returning home after an afternoon of shopping, Aunt Bertha was waiting for her. She suspected she had other plans and wanted to put an end to them. "The ladies are coming over today. I need you to tend to us later."

"Oh, Aunt Bertha, I'm going out to dinner with a friend." Pauline started to fidget with the bag she was holding.

Her aunt spotted it. "With who? That guy with the car?"

Pauline nodded yes and couldn't stop herself from smiling.

"No you're not. I need you here tonight. And you won't need whatever is in that bag you're holding."

"But, Aunt—"

"No buts, end of discussion," Aunt Bertha said smirking as she walked away. "I have to get ready, they'll be here soon. Go get everything set up now."

Pauline reluctantly started to set up the table for the card game. She was disappointed but afraid to push back. She couldn't afford to move out. Not yet at least.

Later that evening, Aunt Bertha and her friends were having another grand time at the card table. As usual, Pauline was busy tending to all the chores, waiting on them hand and foot. She lost track of time until she heard a knock on the front door. "Pauline, get that," her aunt yelled out. Walking toward the door, Pauline suddenly realized it must be Walter. With the number of tasks her aunt doled out, she never told him she couldn't go. She was mortified to see his huge grin when she opened the door.

"Hello, Pauline. Are you ready?"

Aunt Bertha bellowed above the ladies voices yelling, "She ain't going nowhere."

Walter's smile disappeared. "Pauline, what's going on?"

Mary overheard the dispute and started to meddle again. Looking at her old friend she said boldly, "Let her go. She's a young girl who needs to get out."

"She needs to take care of us." Bertha shot a sharp look at her friend.

Mary stood up and approached the door. She smiled when she saw Walter, clearly approving. "Wow, what a handsome young man. You go, Pauline. I'll deal with your aunt."

"No, it's okay. I don't have to go." Pauline didn't want any trouble with her aunt.

"Yes you do. Give me the apron and go already."

Walter looked at her warmly. For the first time, Pauline really noticed how handsome he was and melted under his gaze. She slowly removed the apron and glanced at her aunt who was laughing along with her friends. Mary grabbed the apron from her.

"Good. Now go and have a nice time. You've been taking care of us for months already." Pauline glanced back at her aunt again.

"Go already. I told you, I'll deal with her." Mary nudged her along.

"Okay. Thank you, Mary, for helping me." Pauline grabbed her coat and purse and walked out with Walter.

Pauline bowed her head so he couldn't see her face. "I'm so sorry you had to see that."

"Is this what your aunt has you do all the time?" He stared at her in disbelief while he helped her put her coat on.

"Well...yes. She always has a chore for me to do." She still was unable to meet his gaze.

"Even while you go to school and work?" he said as they started to walk down the stairs. He wondered what more this woman could endure.

"Yes," Pauline whispered. Neither one of them spoke during the car ride to the restaurant. Pauline gazed out the passenger window wondering what her aunt would make her do as punishment for leaving.

Pulling up in front of a fancy, upscale restaurant, Pauline suddenly realized she never changed her clothes.

"Walter, I'm sorry. I forgot to change my clothes. I bought something new to wear today, but with all the commotion at the house, I never changed." She looked down at her faded dress. "I can't go in there looking like this. I'll be mortified."

"You look beautiful." He meant it. "No one will be looking at us. It's one of my favorite restaurants. I come here all the time and I've been dying to take you."

Pauline didn't want to let him down. He was always so kind and understanding. Reluctantly, she agreed.

The maître d' greeted Walter with a friendly smile as he affectionately shook his hand. It was obvious to Pauline he was a regular. As the man helped her remove her coat, he noticed her simple, faded dress. Disapproving, he raised his eyebrows and looked her over before escorting them to a cozy table in the corner. Pauline looked around studying the décor. It was her first time in a restaurant with linen tablecloths and napkins. A rosebud and small candle were positioned in the center of each table. The candle's flicker added to the room's warmth and ambiance. Even though the lighting was dim, Pauline was self-conscious about her clothing. She noticed a few couples from other tables staring at them while giggling.

"Is it me or are those couples looking our way?"

Walter did notice, but didn't want her to feel uncomfortable. He knew Pauline looked out of place, but he didn't care. He was just glad to be with her and tried to cover-up the reason.

"No, maybe they just had too much to drink." Trying to change the subject, he said, "So, tell me about your parents. What do you remember most about them?"

Pauline looked down and started fidgeting with her napkin.

Walter noticed she was uncomfortable and said, "I'm sorry, we don't have to talk about this if you don't want to."

"It's okay." She looked up to meet his gaze. "My mother was a fabulous lady who pushed us to study. All she tried to do was protect me and my little sister from our father."

"Your father? Why, was he bad?" Walter prepared himself for what he might hear next.

Pauline didn't answer, but nodded yes. She was afraid of what he might think if he knew the truth. She didn't want to talk about it with him, not yet at least.

Walter sensed she was getting upset, so he changed the topic…or so he thought. "What made you decide to go into nursing?"

Pauline choked up. A tear formed in the corner of her eye. She turned away so he wouldn't see. He did.

"There I go again, being too nosy. How about we talk about something else?" He was remarkably patient.

"How about you and your family?" Pauline asked.

"Okay, my father passed away from lung cancer. It was very difficult for me to watch. From that point on, all I ever wanted to do was to help people." As Pauline listened, the other couples were no longer a distraction. Walter was all that mattered to her at that moment. "My mother took it hard. I don't think she'll ever get over it. She drinks a lot."

"Do you still live with her?"

"I'm her only child. I'm afraid to move out. I think it will devastate her to be alone."

Pauline took a sip of wine, and then another shortly after. Walter teased. "Take it easy with that, it's very strong." He tried to lighten the mood.

"I don't get out much," Pauline confessed and started to laugh. "I know it shows."

Later that evening, Walter didn't want to say goodbye. He insisted on walking her to the front door of the apartment. Pauline was giddy from drinking too much wine and enjoying the attention from this kind man.

"I had a great time. Thank you for dinner."

"How about we do it again next Saturday?" Walter jumped on the opportunity to see her again.

"I would like that."

"Okay!" Walter's eyes sparkled with joy.

Pauline didn't move. She was hypnotized by his charm and good looks. She stood staring at him, when suddenly, Walter leaned in closer. Their lips touched. Sparks flew. Pauline's first kiss was magical and all that she imagined. Their eyes remained glued on each other as he pulled away. The sound of a door opening caused Pauline to step back from him. Her aunt stood in the doorway scowling. "I think it's late enough, get inside young lady."

"Good evening, ma'am." Walter smiled and bowed his head, still feeling the effects of their first kiss.

Aunt Bertha didn't acknowledge him and walked into the apartment. Walter watched Pauline go through the doorway and as she slowly closed the door, their eyes locked until it was completely shut. He stood there for a few seconds longer, not ready to leave just yet.

Inside, Pauline was surprised to see her aunt staring at her with an annoyed look. She spat at her niece, "Don't ever disrespect me again in front of my friends or you can find somewhere else to live." Pauline looked down and didn't say anything. "Do you understand me?"

"Yes." Pauline looked up to face her callous aunt.

∽✑∾

CHAPTER 18

Josephine's Time Is Now

While at the orphanage, Josephine and Sister Sarah sat in the front office deep in conversation. There's a small bag by Josephine's feet filled with all her worldly possessions. At seventeen years old, she didn't have many belongings. Anxiously she fiddled with a sealed envelope, flicking the corners as they talked. "I just don't have any interest in going to college like my sister," Josephine said to Sister Sarah almost apologetically.

"Are you sure you're ready to leave?" Sister Sarah thought it was too soon. The country was still in an economic depression and she wished Josephine would stay in the orphanage another year.

"It's time. I'm ready to work and make money."

"Why don't you go to New York and get a job near Pauline?" Sister Sarah didn't like the idea of her being on her own, even though she arranged for a job close to the orphanage. The nun was still concerned since it wasn't the same as being under her watchful eye. "I'm sure your aunt will take you in. It would be better than working in the diner across the street. At least Pauline would be around."

"No, that's okay. I'll stay in Lodi for now. I don't want to become a servant for my aunt like my sister has become."

Sister Sarah's eyes started to well up at the thought of Josephine leaving. There was nothing she could say. It was evident her mind was made up. Sister Sarah reached for Josephine's hands and grasped them. She stared into her eyes for a moment remembering, like it was yesterday, the young frightened girl being dropped off by her drunken father. Standing before her now was a determined young lady. She pulled her in tight for a long hug. Josephine threw her arms around the nun as tears streamed down her face. She didn't want to say goodbye, but it was time.

"I can't thank you enough for all you've done for me and my sister. I'll never forget you."

The nun couldn't control her emotions. She wiped the tears from her face as she said, "Don't forget to ask for Thomas. He's a nice man. He'll help you." Josephine nodded and handed her the envelope.

"Is this a letter for your sister?"

"Yes, I want her to know I left."

"I'll be happy to send it for you."

They hugged one last time before Josephine picked up her bag and walked out the door.

Sister Sarah watched as she exited the front gate. "Don't worry, dear, I'll be checking on you," she muttered to herself as she made the sign of the cross.

Josephine strolled down the sidewalk to cross the street to the diner. She wasn't sure what to expect. She looked around taking everything in. Although she lived in the orphanage for eleven years, she hardly went beyond the front gate. She was on her own for the first time and in new surroundings. She grabbed the handle to the diner door and sighed deeply before opening it. With little effort, the door swung open and she stepped inside. She took it all in. The black and white checkered floor and the bright chrome table and chairs were a sharp contrast to the wood finishing in the orphanage. It was glaringly bright and excessively loud. Workers were busy bustling around waiting on patrons who sat at the counter and in booths. Taking another deep breath she wondered what she had gotten herself into.

The owner, a short stocky man, peered out from behind the counter to look at Josephine. He immediately noticed the worried look on her face. He had been expecting her one day. Wide eyed, she was easy to pick out of a crowd wearing faded, outdated clothes carrying a small bag.

The man approached her and said, "Josephine?"

"Yes. Are you Thomas?"

"Yes." He motioned to the first booth. "Let's sit here."

Josephine slid into the booth and sat opposite Thomas. She was very quiet and reserved, not like her usual, bubbly self.

Thomas noticed her uneasiness and began to talk. "Sister Sarah mentioned you might also need a place to stay?" Josephine nodded yes but didn't speak.

"Okay, I have rooms available in the house behind the diner. Many of the other workers live there too. You can have one if you like."

"That would be great." She smiled for the first time since she arrived.

"Good then, I'll deduct the rent from your wages." Thomas didn't hesitate and got right into the details.

"Rent? What's rent?"

Surprised, Thomas said, "It's a fee for the room."

"Oh, I'm sorry." Feeling more at ease, she giggled. "I never rented anything before."

Thomas started to get a glimpse of her bubbly personality. He felt very sorry for her and said, "I know you're just starting out. I'll give you a break for a few months until you start getting a handle of things around here."

"Thank you. That's very kind of you, sir. I can start now if you'd like?" Josephine was eager to begin work since she didn't have any money or anywhere else to go.

Thomas called out to one of the waitresses. "Flo, come here please."

Snapping her gum and twirling her pen, the waitress approached the table. "What do you want?"

"This is Josephine, a new girl. Show her around and teach her what to do." Thomas looked at Josephine. "Flo's the best. She'll take good care of you."

Josephine shadowed Flo straight through the dinner rush. She couldn't believe how busy it was. In between helping customers, Flo jabbered on that ever since the depression hit, the diner business boomed and they were always busy. Eager to make money, Josephine wanted to learn and watched Flo carefully so she did everything she was asked to do.

At first, Thomas was concerned that Josephine was too quiet and shy, but after carefully watching her through the dinner rush, he was pleased with how she interacted with the customers. Impressed, he whispered to another waitress, "She's a real hustler. She's going to do just fine here."

After her shift was over, Thomas showed Josephine to her room. It was a short walk from the diner. "You did a great job today." Thomas honestly believed it. "You'll shadow Flo for a few more days and then you'll be ready to be on your own."

"Oh, thank you." Josephine laughed as she said, "It's hard work, but at least I'm no longer scrubbing floors all day."

They entered the house and Thomas showed her the room. It was small and dark, but suited Josephine just fine. She didn't need much. She was mentally and physically exhausted from the day's events and plopped onto the bed as soon as Thomas left. She was grateful for his kindness. "Pauli, I miss you. Please watch over me, especially now," she whispered into the darkness. And like every night before, she ritualistically peeked over to look for her in the next bed. Overcome with emotion, she cried herself to sleep. A new chapter had begun.

CHAPTER 19

❧

I Care

Pauline kept up with her rigorous routine for months. She attended school during the day, worked in the evening, tended to her aunt's chores, and saw Walter whenever she had spare time. She got used to always being exhausted. She wasn't going to let it get her down.

It was a crisp autumn evening. She welcomed the fresh, cool air after being in the hot factory for hours. She daydreamed about her diploma and how close she was to receiving it as she dragged herself down the sidewalk for her long walk home. She was halfway through her schooling and had just a little while more to go of the exhausting schedule. While she was deep in thought, a car approached from behind jolting her back to reality. Ever since her episode with the derelict, she was easily spooked. Her nerves eased and face softened when she saw Walter's car slowing down.

"I can't have you doing this every night," she said hiding her relief as he got out of the car. She was frightened since the incident but didn't want him to know.

"I want to. I can't let you walk the streets alone, especially after what happened."

Pauline noticed his genuine concern and paused before answering. She liked having someone take care and pamper her but still wanted to maintain her independence.

"I'll be fine, Walter."

"Please, let me drive you. I'll just feel better."

Tilting her head and smiling, Pauline walked to the passenger side. Walter held the door open for her as she got into the car and then slammed the metal door shut.

Pauline looked over at Walter as he slid into the driver's seat. Her heart fluttered when she saw his handsome face. Gaining her composure she said, "Thank you for doing this."

Walter looked at her tenderly. "What kind of man would I be if I let you walk the streets alone?"

"It's not your responsibility." Pauline shot him a look, naïve to his true feelings.

"I know it's not. I do it because I care." They rode in silence until they arrived at Pauline's apartment.

"You don't need to walk me to the door. I'm fine from here," Pauline said as he opened the car door.

Pretending he didn't hear her, Walter walked her inside and up the three flights of stairs. They paused when they got to the door. Turning to face each other, they had the same glow and sparkle in their eyes as the first night. Any tension they felt from the car ride was now gone as Walter looked intensely into Pauline's eyes. He leaned in closer to her. Their lips touched. They were unaware of anything else at that moment. They didn't hear the door open or see Aunt Bertha standing there. Aunt Bertha loudly coughed as she leaned against the doorway with her arms folded across her chest.

Pauline nervously pulled back. Walter very calmly smiled broadly and tipped his head like a gentleman. "Good evening, ma'am."

Aunt Bertha brushed it off and turned toward Pauline. "It's late. Get inside."

Pauline looked back at Walter who was still brimming from ear to ear. "Thank you again, Walter," she said and turned to enter the apartment. She watched him walk away as she closed the door.

"You're a naive young girl. He's up to no good," Aunt Bertha barked at Pauline the moment the door completely closed.

"He's a gentleman, Aunt Bertha. Why else would he go out of his way to pick me up at the factory and drive me home at night?" Pauline coolly responded.

"Why do you think?" Aunt Bertha snickered. "He's after one thing. I don't want you to see him anymore."

Pauline didn't acknowledge or respond to her aunt's demand. "I have chores to do," Pauline said and she quickly walked into the kitchen. Aunt Bertha smiled deviously knowing that she had planted the seed.

The next day Pauline was thinking about what her aunt had said. Is he really after only one thing? She was quieter than usual at lunch. Dolly guessed something was up. "What gives, you barely touched your food?"

"I'm just tired."

Dolly didn't believe her. "Pauline, I'm your friend. You can tell me anything."

Pauline wasn't used to having people care about her. She was trying to navigate her new relationships and it was more challenging than she expected. Plus, she really didn't know what to do about her aunt and Walter. She needed some friendly advice. Looking up at Dolly, she decided to confide in her. "My aunt wants me to stop seeing Walter. She says he's only after one thing."

Dolly couldn't contain her surprise. "Walter? He is the most respected doctor here." Dolly thought further for a second. She knew about the chores and demands Aunt Bertha continuously put on her friend. She suspected that Pauline's aunt had an ulterior motive, even though Pauline never let on. In that moment, Dolly came up with a plan to help her. "How about you move in with me? We can split the rent."

"I'm barely able to pay the tuition. I could never afford it." Pauline rested her chin on her hand and looked down at her tray full of food. She wanted desperately to move out of her aunt's apartment.

Dolly pressed on. "You need to get away from her. She's controlling your life now."

"I would love to, Dolly, but it's just not an option for me right now. I can't afford it."

Pauline noticed Millie glaring at them from another table. Dolly followed Pauline's gaze. Millie quickly turned around the moment she saw Dolly. Trying to change the topic Pauline said, "I think she hates me now."

"Don't worry about her. She'll get over it," Dolly replied.

"Hello, ladies, is this a private conversation or can I join you for lunch?" Walter stood their grinning while waiting for an answer before sitting down.

Dolly replied before Pauline had a chance to answer, "Of course you can join us."

Millie brooded at the other table. She still had a crush on Walter and wished she was sitting with the three of them.

A nurse approached the table and handed Pauline an envelope. "This is addressed to you, Pauline. It came to the front office." Pauline took the letter from the nurse and thanked her for delivering it. Her eyes lit up when she saw it was from her sister. She ripped opened the envelope and slid out the letter. She read to herself.

Dear Pauli,

I'm leaving the orphanage to go to work across the street at the diner. Sister Sarah said that it's very busy and I should make good money. I just don't have any interest in going to college. I hope you're doing well and just wanted to let you know where I am. I miss you.

Love,

Josie

Tears rolled down Pauline's cheeks as she read the letter. Seeing Pauline cry, Walter and Dolly were alarmed. "What's wrong?" Walter asked.

"Nothing. It's from my sister. I'm just glad she's okay." She dabbed her face with her napkin to dry it. She didn't want anyone to see her cry, especially Walter.

"Where is she?" Dolly asked.

"She's still in New Jersey. She got a job working at a diner."

Pauline folded the letter and tucked it away in her pocket. She was glad she was still close to the orphanage and Sister Sarah.

Later that day, Pauline couldn't focus in class. She was thinking about her sister. Although she wished that Josephine had continued with her schooling, she understood why she left the orphanage. She wanted her to know and started to draft a letter.

Dear Josie,

I received your letter and am so glad you're okay. I worry about you all the time. I wish you were here. Although I would rather you finish your schooling and go to college, I'm happy that you're doing well.

I met a nice doctor named Walter. I can't wait for you to meet him. I really want to move out of Aunt Bertha's apartment. All she does is make me do chores and tries to stop me from seeing him. I can't afford to though. Maybe one day.

Well anyway, I love you.

Pauli

Lost in thought, the teacher startled Pauline. "Miss Roka, are you paying attention or daydreaming again?" The teacher stopped writing on the blackboard and stared at her.

"Yes, ma'am, I'm paying attention." Pauline looked at the teacher while sliding the letter under her book.

CHAPTER 20

∾

Moving Forward

It was Saturday night. Walter and Pauline entered the restaurant they had frequented every week. At least the maître d' smiled at her cordially now, even though he still wondered what a successful, good looking man saw in Pauline. As regulars they were both greeted warmly, unlike when they dined together on their first date. As usual, they were ushered to the table in the corner of the room. It was their table. Pauline was more at ease now and Walter noticed. He gazed into her eyes and smiled while reaching for her hand. "I would like you to meet my mother."

She stared at him in disbelief. "Are you sure, Walter? It's kind of soon."

"No it's not." He pulled his hand away as the smile erased from his face. "Unless of course, you don't want to."

She didn't want to hurt him since he was always so patient with her. Pauline hesitated before replying, "Okay, I would love to."

"Are you sure?" Walter picked up on her hesitation.

"I just never met anyone's mother before. What if she doesn't like me?"

"Just be yourself, you'll be fine. She'll love you, I know it." He reached for her hand again and softly squeezed it.

The rest of the night they casually laughed, ate, and enjoyed each other's company. Even though she didn't let on, Pauline was still very concerned about meeting his mother.

The following Saturday, Walter picked up Pauline to take her to his home in Bronxville, New York. It was an affluent village just under five miles from New Rochelle. Although the two communities were close in proximity, they were worlds apart. Residents who lived in Bronxville had plenty of money and their large houses and pristinely manicured lawns were a snap shot into their wealth and privileged life.

It was a beautiful day. The bright sunshine added even more splendor to the upscale neighborhood. Pauline fidgeted with her dress as she quietly gazed out the car window. Walter drove slowly through his neighborhood pointing out different landmarks as they went by. Pulling into a long driveway and stopping the car in front of a sprawling stone colonial, Pauline stared in amazement. "It's enormous. What is this place?"

Walter helped her out of the car. Turning to face her he held both her hands and said, "This is my house."

Pauline gasped. "Your house?"

"Yes, it is. Let's go inside, mother is waiting for us." It was the largest house Pauline had ever seen. She stood there dazed and didn't move. Walter took her hand and threaded it through his—he didn't let go. They strolled together, arm in arm, to the front door. The fragrance from the freshly cut lawn and blooming flowers overtook Pauline's senses. Everything was perfect. It was stunning.

Walter pushed open the front door. He paused to allow her to enter first. She stepped into a large foyer and caught her breath upon seeing an ornate chandelier hanging above a striking art deco, geometrically designed floor. And on the steps of a grand, wooden staircase, a middle-aged woman stood wearing an exquisite, long-waisted dress that flowed gently along her curves to a slightly flared bottom. Pursing her lips, she held a long, silver cigarette holder as the smoke rose above her head. She watched them enter without saying a word.

Pauline started smoothing out her simple dress as Walter softly nudged her forward. "Go ahead, Pauline."

Pauline took a few steps and the sound of her shoes clanked against the ceramic floor. She smiled at the woman as she walked closer. Nodding in return, the woman turned to walk to the sitting room without uttering a word. Walter tried to get his mother's attention. "Mother, this is my friend Pauline." The woman stopped and turned toward them. Walter continued the introduction and said, "Pauline, this is my mother Marion."

Sensing her disapproval, Pauline meekly smiled and offered her hand. "It's nice to meet you, ma'am."

Narrowing her gaze, Marion scanned her dress before extending her hand. Pauline's fear was becoming a reality.

The three entered the sitting room. Walter sat next to Pauline who was fidgeting with her clothes trying to get comfortable. She had never been in a situation like this before. She felt completely out of place. They sipped from tea cups made of bone china and sat in imported wingback chairs. Walter fussed over Pauline, trying to help her feel at ease.

Marion noticed the attention and concern Walter had for Pauline. She wasn't pleased and started peppering her with questions. "So what town are you from, Pauline?"

"Lodi, New Jersey, ma'am."

"What does your father do for a living?"

Pauline took a sip of tea and slowly placed her cup down to gather her thoughts. Walter jumped in noticing her discomfort. "Mother, what's with all the questions?"

Marion shot her son a look. "Darling, we're just getting acquainted with each other."

"My father works in a shoe factory," Pauline said.

"As a supervisor?"

"No, ma'am."

"Oh gosh... an hourly worker? How can you afford to go to nursing school?" Marion continued to probe.

"I work in a girdle factory to pay for my tuition."

"You're a...a factory worker?"

"Mother!" Walter was mortified. He turned to Pauline. "Let's go. Come on, we're leaving."

Pauline always knew she was out of her league, but Walter made it easy for her to forget. It wasn't until today that she realized how completely different their upbringings actually were. Standing up to leave, she turned to Marion and said, "It was nice to meet you."

Marion nodded but didn't respond. "Mother, we'll talk about this later," Walter said before storming out with Pauline.

Neither one of them spoke during the car ride home. Gazing out the window, Pauline was awed by the affluent community. She imagined what it must have been like for Walter growing up and playing on the large, sprawling lawns with friends, riding bicycles down the street, and having family dinners with plenty of food on the table. She was the first to speak. Without breaking her gaze she said, "Obviously, your mother doesn't like me."

"She's just being protective. I'm her only child. I'm all she has right now." Walter defended his mother.

"No, she looks down on me. I'm not good enough for you."

Walter knew she had a right to feel that way after his mother's behavior. He reached out to hold her hand. "Yes you are. It's what matters to me."

"I just don't understand, Walter. You come from money, you have all this, and I have nothing. Why are you so interested in me?"

"I told you already. I think you're fascinating. It has nothing to do with money." He chose his words carefully. "I never had to struggle like you. Look at all you've gone through to become a nurse. I've never met anyone like you before."

Pauline didn't reply. She had a lot to think about.

While at work that evening, Pauline couldn't stop thinking about Marion's behavior. Preoccupied with what to do next and unable to concentrate, she fell behind on her count and needed a moment to regroup. She tucked her hands into her sweater pockets and felt an envelope. It was the letter she had received from Josephine earlier that day and didn't have time to read. She opened it close to her body to not draw any attention to what she was doing. Money fell onto her lap. She swiftly hid it in her bra and read the letter.

Dear Pauli,

I'm working day and night and making good tips. The customers really like me and the diner is busy all the time. There's no depression here and it sure beats scrubbing floors. Please take this money and get away from Aunt Bertha. I know if our roles were reversed you would do the same for me. Every month I will send you money so you don't have to worry. Just take it and don't be ashamed. I want to help. It's the least I can do after you protected me for so many years when we were young.

I miss you.

Love, Josie

Overwhelmed, Pauline held her head in her hand and sobbed. Wiping the tears from her eyes so she could get back to work, she looked up to see the manager standing over her with folded arms. Nervously, Pauline slid the letter in her pocket and placed a piece of fabric on the machine.

The following day in the hospital cafeteria, Pauline confided to Dolly that her sister wanted to send her money each month.

Dolly exclaimed, "That's great. With your sister's help you can move in with me whenever you're ready."

Pauline played with her food. "I can't do this to my sister."

"You're crazy. This is your chance to get away from your aunt who only cares about herself. Look what she puts you through."

"It's not right for my sister to have to pay for me."

"She's doing this on her own, Pauline. You didn't ask her for anything." Dolly tried to knock some sense into her, knowing how proud and independent she was.

Deep down Pauline wanted to move out of her aunt's apartment. She was tired and had enough of her aunt's selfish demands.

A few weeks later more money arrived from Josephine. Pauline knew this was her time and her opportunity to break free from the clutches of her aunt. She paced the apartment floor unsure of how her aunt would react to her news. Taking a deep breath, she straightened her back, lifted her head up high, and approached her. "Aunt Bertha, I have to tell you something." Aunt Bertha nodded, but didn't look up from the magazine she was reading. "I have an opportunity to move in with a friend from school."

Caught off guard, Aunt Bertha lifted her head and said, "You're crazy. Who's gonna look out for you?"

"I just can't do this anymore. Go to school, work, and then do chores all night. I'm exhausted all the time."

Aunt Bertha snapped back sarcastically, "It's not the chores, it's the doctor that's clouded your mind."

"This has nothing to do with him. He doesn't even know. It would be easier for me." Pauline tried desperately to get her aunt to see her perspective.

"Don't you understand? He will eventually leave you. You're just a peasant girl compared to him." She smirked when she saw the color drain from Pauline's face. That was cruel, even for her.

For the first time, Pauline stood up to her aunt. "That's not true. I'm going to make something of myself. You'll see." Now that she had something to fall back on she wasn't backing down. Not today.

"You just don't get it. Some people are fortunate and some aren't. Your path in life has already been chosen for you."

Pauline refused to believe that. She spent her whole life beating the odds. "It can't be that simple. It just can't."

"It is." Her aunt threw her head back and let out a sinister laugh. Staring at her niece she said, "In the end, your life is already planned out. The odds are stacked against you. The sooner you understand this, the better off you'll be."

"No, you're wrong this time. Just because you let life bring you down, doesn't mean I have to." Pauline spat back. "I refuse to end up like you!"

Aunt Bertha was furious. Her face turned red as she stood up from the couch. "You're so ungrateful! After all I've done for you, this is how you talk to me?"

Pauline had pushed too far. She knew it, but couldn't control all the pent up emotions any longer. She stepped back as her aunt approached her, uncertain of what was coming next. Her aunt got close to her face which brought flashbacks of her father's vicious temper. Pauline took another step back. "Take your small possessions and your pathetic self… and get out. Now!"

CHAPTER 21

❧

Hanging On

It was a typical morning in the institution. Ada waited for her breakfast while saying her morning prayers. Lena drifted in. Her face was drawn, her body dragged, it was clear to Ada that something was troubling her. She wasn't her normal, lively self. Ada asked, "Lena, what's wrong?"

"I'm beside myself with worry. One of my daughters is very ill. The doctors say it's a rare disease. There's not much hope." Lena could hardly get the words out before sobbing into her hands.

Ada made the sign of the cross and clutched her rosary beads. She said, "May God be with her and give her strength."

Upon gaining her composure Lena stated, "I'm taking a leave of absence to care for her. I'm so sorry I haven't been able to visit your daughters yet."

Ada reached out to hold Lena's hand. "You've already been a blessing to me. You take care of your little girl." Ada bowed her head down knowing there was probably no hope of seeing her daughters again.

Lena noticed Ada's change in demeanor and tried to lift her spirits. She said, "I promise. As soon as she gets better, I'll find them."

Ada looked up. "You go and care for your daughter. That's your most important concern for now. At least I know where my daughters are because of you."

Lena didn't know what to say. She leaned over and hugged Ada tight as tears continued to flow down her cheeks.

Later that evening, Ada sat alone in bed. The stillness of the night was unbearable. She already missed Lena. They had become close friends. She rolled onto her side and lifted her locket from the nightstand. She stared at the girls' picture for a moment before breaking down into tears. Her hopes had been shattered. "My precious, little girls, I'm so sorry," she said out loud before falling asleep.

After the argument with her aunt, Pauline packed her few belongings and stormed out for good. She walked to the boarding house where Dolly lived. In all their time together as friends, she had never been to the house. It was everything she had imagined. A few steps led up to a small white porch with chipped paint. It was quaint, only two floors high. It looked perfect to Pauline. And more importantly, she felt liberated for the first time since she arrived in New York. At last, she would get some sleep.

Dolly greeted her at the door with a huge smile. "Finally," she said and led her into the house. Pauline looked around at the simple furnishings and small kitchen. It was all she needed and she couldn't have been more pleased.

Dolly brought her upstairs to the bedrooms. As they walked down the creaky hallway, Millie came bursting out of her room. "Dolly, is that you?" She stopped short when she saw Pauline. "What's she doing here?"

"She's living here now. She's going to share my room with me."

Millie shook her head, but didn't say a word. The boarding house was her alone time with Dolly. She stormed back into her room and slammed the door. Pauline darted her eyes toward Dolly who didn't give it a second thought. "Come on, it's fine."

Dolly continued down the hallway. Pauline followed, but looked back toward Millie's door. She didn't want to cause any more trouble. She entered the last bedroom where two cots were arranged side by side in the middle of a small room.

"It's the only way I was able to fit it for both of us. I hope it's okay?" Dolly wanted to make sure her friend would be comfortable since she always had it so tough. She wanted living together to be easy for Pauline. What Dolly didn't realize was that Pauline had slept like this for years while at the orphanage.

Pauline was concerned that the new arrangement would be an inconvenience for her friend. "Dolly, you don't have to do this. I'm taking your bed away. You shouldn't have to sleep on a cot."

"We're friends. I want to. This is what friends do for one another. I cleared out a drawer for you and the closet is over there. Put your things away and let's get something to eat. I'm starved."

"I'm so touched by everything you did. Honestly, I don't know what else to say."

"Just say you're hungry too." Dolly nudged her arm as they both laughed together.

While Pauline was settling into her cozy new home, Walter and his mother sat together in their sprawling living room. Walter worked extra hours that week filling in for some doctors who were out of town. He came home tired each evening and went straight to bed. Tonight was the night he planned on talking to his mother about her rude behavior toward Pauline. It had been festering inside him for days, but he barely spoke a word over dinner. He collected his thoughts first because it wasn't going to be an easy conversation.

As they each sipped an after-dinner drink, Marion sensed his displeasure and wanted to say her peace. She didn't beat around the bush and got straight to the point. "She's no good for you, Walter."

"Why? What do you mean?" He wasn't pleased he was forced into the discussion on her terms.

"She has nothing to offer you. She's poor."

"Why does that matter? She's studying to be a nurse now."

"And where's her family? She has no family values."

"All that doesn't matter to me, mother. I care for who she is, not what she has." Walter stood up and started to pace.

"Feelings don't pay the bills. Money does. There are plenty of appropriate girls in this town who would jump at the chance to be with you. A girl like Millie, who was raised properly, would be a much better match. Millie understands how to be a proper wife and behave appropriately. You should be with someone who can maintain the lifestyle you deserve." Marion tried to reason with her son.

"I deserve? I deserve it no more than Pauline or anyone else for that matter. I'm not looking for a spoiled rich girl. I want someone with heart and drive like Pauline." Walter had never crossed his mother before, but he was determined to defend Pauline. He only wanted to be with her.

Listening to her son, Marion realized how much he actually cared for Pauline. It unsettled her. She paused for a moment knowing he was not giving in. Marion needed to find another way to get through to him. She finished her nightcap, stood up, and looked right at him. With a steady tone she said, "Just know, I'll never approve of her." She walked out of the room leaving him to his thoughts.

Walter screamed, "It's my life. I get to choose who I want to be with."

CHAPTER 22

❧

Until the Bitter End

It was the beginning of May. Another fall and winter had passed with the same daily grind. Dolly and Pauline had become even closer friends over the past semester. They were inseparable. Strolling down the hospital hallway arm in arm Pauline said, "I can't believe we're graduating soon. It doesn't feel real to me. It's like it's all a dream."

"You worked hard for this, Pauline. I'm so proud of you." Dolly affectionately bumped into her as they walked.

"You made it easier by taking me in. I could never thank you enough." Pauline squeezed herself closer to her.

"You should thank your sister. She made it possible by sending you money. I had it easy. I got to live with my best friend."

Walter walked down the hall toward them. He grinned when he spotted them walking together. He was glad Pauline found such a good friend. They all stopped when they got close to each other.

Walter stole a quick kiss from Pauline and said, "I'll pick you up later after work. Gotta run now." He hurried down the hall and nodded to Millie who watched from a distance. Even after all this time, she was still annoyed.

Pauline and Dolly noticed Millie staring at Walter as he walked by. Pauline still felt badly for Millie. "I'm sorry that you're not friends anymore. It's all because of me."

Without hesitating Dolly replied, "We're learning that life is short. We can't worry about jealousy. It will drag us down."

Pauline smiled. She was grateful for her good friend.

Back in the institution, Ada was in her bed extremely weak and pale. Her eyes were barely opened. Lena walked in after being away for six months. Noticing the extreme difference since she had last seen Ada, Lena dashed to the bed.

"Oh my, what has happened to you?"

"I think my time is near," she said briefly opening her eyes to look at Lena. Closing them again she asked, "Never mind me, how's your daughter?"

Tears streamed down Lena's cheeks. She attempted to quickly wipe them away, but she couldn't stop crying. "She passed on. My little angel is gone."

Ada felt her loss. Tears also rolled down her cheeks. "I'm so sorry. She was too young to join God. No parent should ever have to endure that pain."

Lena reached behind Ada's head and tilted it up. With her other hand, she placed a cup to her mouth. "Drink this. I need you to get better. I'm now more determined than ever to get your daughters here. I know firsthand how hard it is for a mother to lose her child."

Ada held Lena's hand. "Don't be concerned with me. You worry about yourself and your family."

Lena looked compassionately at her friend's despondent state. She knew there wasn't much time left. She said to Ada, "Can I ask you a question? There is something that has been bothering me for some time now."

"Yes, of course you can."

"Was it really depression that made your husband bring you here or was it something else?"

Ada closed her eyes. Then opening them she said, "Harry didn't like that I wanted more out of life for my daughters. He thought they should just cook and clean like me."

"So the reason on your application isn't true?"

Ada shook her head no. "The girls' studies were most important to me. I wanted them to be educated so they could choose their own path in life."

Lena always suspected there was more to Ada's story. She wanted to make sure Ada's daughters knew the truth about their mother's wishes, but was concerned that Ada had given up hope. Surmising that there wasn't much time left, Lena whispered to her as she quietly rested, "You just hang in there a little while longer. I'll find them."

That evening, Lena arrived at the Lodi Orphanage. She banged on the front door anxious to find the girls. The door slowly opened. Sister Sarah stood by the doorway. "Yes, may I help you?"

"Hi, I'm looking for the Roka sisters. I understand you might be caring for them."

"And you are?" Sister Sarah cautiously inquired.

"I care for their mother at an institution. I've been looking for them for quite some time now."

Sister Sarah's eyes opened wide. "Please, come in." Lena entered and followed the nun, relieved that she might have found the right place. "This is a blessing. How is she?"

"Recently, she took a turn for the worse. I would love the girls to visit her before…" Lena looked down, she couldn't finish the sentence after just losing her own little girl.

"We did care for the girls for a long time but they are no longer here. The oldest daughter, Pauline, left for nursing school in New York and Josephine just recently started working."

Lena was distraught by this news. "I waited too long. It's all my fault."

Sister Sarah couldn't reveal where the girls were, but she knew how much they missed their mother. "You look tired. Why don't you go across the street and get something hot to drink. It will do you some good before your travels home. Be sure to ask for Josephine, she's the best waitress they have."

Lena perked up and hugged the nun long and hard. "Thank you so much."

Sister Sarah blessed her and said, "Thank you for all your efforts. This would truly be a miracle for them after all these years."

Lena raced across the street and entered the front door of the diner. Trying to picture the little girl in Ada's locket, Lena glanced around looking for a grown up version of Josephine. She wasn't able to recognize her.

Thomas approached Lena. "One, ma'am?"

"Well, um, actually I'm wondering if you could help me. I'm looking for Josephine."

Thomas always protected his workers. Not knowing who she was or what she wanted from her, he took a step back to look her over. "What do you want with her?"

"I care for her mother. I'm trying to reunite them after all these years."

Raising his eyebrows, Thomas couldn't believe what he just heard. Knowing Josephine's history, he called out to her. "Josephine, please come here for a minute."

Josephine stood at a table taking a customer's order. She nodded to him. Lena was overwhelmed with joy that she finally found one of the girls. Josephine approached them. "Yes." Thomas nodded to Lena to share her great news.

Lena couldn't contain her happiness. She got right to the point and said, "You don't know me, but I've been caring for your mother all these years."

Shocked by the sudden news, Josephine's pad fell to the ground. "We never knew where she was or if she was still alive. Our father didn't tell us anything when he dropped us off at the orphanage."

"She's been in an institution. Unfortunately, only your father can sign her out. He never did. I've been searching for you girls for some time now. Your mother never knew what happened to you."

"I'm so glad you found me. It sounds like you went through a lot of trouble. Why would you do this?"

"Your mother has been so worried about you girls." Lena looked down to compose herself. "I know what it's like to lose a child and can imagine what has been going through your mother's mind." Josephine was still trying to digest the news as she bent down to pick up her pad. "Do you know where Pauline is?" Lena asked.

"Yes." Josephine lit up, beaming with pride. "She's almost finished with nursing school in New York."

"I will certainly tell your mother. Please, could you and your sister visit her as soon as possible?" Lena wrote the institution's name and address on Josephine's pad. "She's not doing well. It would mean the world to her."

"Yes, I'm going to write Pauli tonight. I promise we'll get there soon." They hugged goodbye as Thomas watched from the distance.

In the meantime, Harry's life didn't change. He perched himself on the same stool every night drinking whiskey with the regulars at his favorite pub. It was a typical evening. He tilted the glass back to down the shot and then slammed the empty glass against the bar. That was his signal to the barmaid for a refill. This night wasn't any different, except he started violently coughing into his sleeve after every shot. It was a deep, troubling cough. His friend noticed his blood-stained sleeve.

"You need to get checked out, Harry. You're bleeding."

"I can see for myself," he barked at his friend. "I don't have money for a doctor right now."

"Your girls should be old enough by now to care for you. Why don't you visit them?"

Harry perked up. He never thought of that. "You're right. I did them a favor by bringing them to the orphanage. They should repay me now."

Even though it was late, Harry stumbled out of the pub determined to get the girls. Once he arrived at the orphanage, he struggled to walk up the stairs, resting after every few steps. When he finally reached the front door, with what little strength he had left, he knocked. No one answered. He banged again harder. Still no one answered. Using all of his strength, he pounded with both hands causing a complete ruckus. In the still of the night, he heard the door unlock. Opening it, Sister Sarah stood there in shock. Annoyed by his presence, she asked curtly, "Mr. Roka?"

"Yeah, that's right."

"What can I do for you? It's late."

Harry tried to enter the orphanage. She didn't move. "I'm here to sign out my daughters."

Detecting his slurred speech and drunken state, she stared at him for a moment before answering. She wanted to choose her words carefully and not test his temper. "I'm sorry, sir, they are no longer here with us. Good night," the nun said as she started to close the door. Annoyed, he slammed his hand against the frame to stop it from closing.

"Where can I find them?" he blurted out.

"They didn't say where they were going. Good night, Mr. Roka, it's late." She tried to close the door again.

Harry stared at her for a moment deciding what to do next. She didn't flinch and held her ground not budging. Without a thank you or acknowledgment, Harry turned to walk away. She watched him stumble down the cement walkway before closing the door. "Please God, watch over them," she said as she locked the door securely.

Harry saw the bright lights from the diner and headed toward it to get a cup of coffee. Barely able to open the front door, he stumbled in, violently coughing into his blood-stained sleeve. Thomas noticed and kept an eye on him. He wanted no trouble tonight.

It wasn't too busy. Harry squinted from the bright lights and started to walk toward the counter. Josephine appeared from the kitchen holding stacks of food. She spotted her father and froze. The dishes crashed to the ground. Thomas raced over. "Josephine, are you all right?" Josephine didn't respond. Her eyes were glued on Harry. Thomas followed her gaze and noticed she was frightened by the disheveled looking drunk who had just entered the diner. Thomas had no idea who he was. Reaching down to pick up the broken plates, he tried talking to her again. "Josephine, what's wrong?"

Josephine didn't move or break her gaze from Harry. Upon hearing the crash, Harry turned toward the sound and locked eyes with his daughter. "You have no right coming here after what you did to our family," Josephine yelled from across the room.

"Josephine, is that you?" Harry was surprised to see his daughter.

"What do you want after all these years?"

"I can't believe you're here. I was looking for you. I just came for a cup of coffee. What a coincidence this is." Harry smirked in delight.

"Who is this?" Thomas asked.

"I'm her father, that's who I am." Harry interjected before Josephine could answer.

Startled, Thomas turned to look at Josephine whose gaze was still fixated on her father.

"Just get out. You're not welcome here." Josephine started to tremble. Realizing that she dropped the dishes, she squatted down to help Thomas clean up the mess.

"Josephine, it's been awhile. I didn't even recognize you." Harry stumbled closer to his daughter as Josephine continued to clean up. Thomas stayed close by her side.

"Awhile? We were in the orphanage for over ten years."

Harry realized she was upset. "How about I come back tomorrow so we can talk?"

Josephine stood up and looked directly at him. "We have nothing to talk about."

"I know it's a lot right now for you to handle. I'll be back tomorrow." Without waiting for a reply, Harry staggered to the front door. He was thrilled he knew where to find her.

"Don't do me any favors," she yelled at him and was furious that he suddenly appeared after all these years. Needing to keep busy, she immediately went back to work. She didn't speak about it, but Thomas watched her closely for the rest of the evening. He knew to keep an eye out for his return the next day. Later that evening, Josephine glanced around while nervously walking home. She wasn't aware that Thomas was watching out for her from a distance. Once safely alone in her room, she broke down in tears. She wondered why her fathered showed up now after all these years.

She tossed and turned all night wondering what he wanted and why he never visited them in the orphanage. Sluggishly, she walked to the diner for the early morning rush, hoping he wouldn't show. Upon entering, she was glad to see it was already fairly busy. She quickly got to work. She thought it would keep her mind occupied, but she couldn't stop glancing toward the front door. Thomas watched from the counter noticing that she was on edge and preoccupied.

True to his word, Harry entered the diner shortly after the morning rush. He paused to make sure Josephine was working before settling into a table. Thomas watched closely while Josephine approached him.

"What do you want?" Josephine was annoyed he came back.

Harry hacked into his sleeve before answering. "I would like you to move back with me."

"I meant to eat? What can I get you?" she replied curtly.

"I know you're mad, but it was the best thing for you two." Harry was angling to play on her sympathy.

"Yeah, how about what you did to mom?"

"You were too young to understand. Your mother was a troubled lady and needed help."

"You and your temper were her problem!" Josephine shouted at him.

"Her sickness wasn't my fault." He kept his voice even.

"She wasn't sick, you –."

"Is everything okay, Josephine?" Thomas noticed she was getting very agitated and hurried toward them. When Josephine didn't respond, Thomas glared at Harry to send a message. "Okay, sir, I think that's enough for today. I have to ask you to leave."

"Leave? This is my daughter. I don't have to go anywhere."

"Just go! Get out!" Josephine was trembling.

"Let's go." Thomas reached to help Harry up. Harry coughed and brushed Thomas' hand away so he could stand up on his own.

"I'll come back another day. I'll give you some time." He smirked at his daughter before walking away.

"Don't bother. I never want to see you again. Stay away from here."

Ignoring his daughter, Harry purposely bumped shoulders with Thomas as he walked passed him. Thomas watched to make sure Harry left the building as Josephine raced into the bathroom. It was all too much for her to handle. First was the news of her mother and now her father's return. Slamming the door closed, she slid down the wall to the floor, covered her face with her hands, and sobbed alone.

"Josephine, are you okay?" Thomas asked through the closed door.

"Yes, just give me one more minute please."

Josephine wiped her tears away, composed herself, and went back to work.

It was a beautiful, sunny day and Lena quickly walked through the institution to Ada's room. She couldn't wait to reveal her good news that she had finally found one of Ada's daughters. She was heartbroken to see her lying in the bed weak and frail. It saddened her to see Ada in this state. Lena placed a glass of water to her lips. Ada took a sip and leaned back.

Lena couldn't contain her happiness any longer and blurted out her news. "I found Josephine. She works at a diner."

"You found my baby. How is she?"

"She's great! I noticed that the owner, Thomas, watches over her."

"How does she look?"

"Beautiful, Ada. She's beautiful. She's got your eyes."

"Did she say anything about Pauline?"

"Yes, Pauline is almost done with nursing school. She's in New York and will be graduating real soon."

Ada closed her eyes as the corner of her mouth curled up happy to hear the good news. A tear fell down her cheek. She whispered so softly that Lena was barely able to hear her, "I'm so relieved they're okay. I've been so worried about them." For the first time, Lena saw Ada's body completely relaxed and content. Lena placed the blanket across Ada's frail frame.

"You get some rest now. I'll check on you later." Lena stepped back and looked at Ada who was quickly deteriorating. She hoped the girls would hurry up and get there soon.

Life for Pauline was getting easier now that she was out from under her aunt's thumb. Although she was still working at the factory to pay for her tuition, she was now able to finally get some sleep. She felt forever indebted to her sister and Dolly for their generosity. At last, she enjoyed her time at nursing school. Every day the threesome, Pauline, Dolly, and Walter, sat at their usual lunch table. It was a typical afternoon when a lady approached. "Pauline, this letter is addressed to you. It came today." Pauline thanked her and tore it open.

"Is that from your sister?" Dolly asked.

Pauline nodded yes. She quickly read it. Like always, tears streamed down her cheeks when she read her sister's letters.

"What's going on? Is everything okay?" Dolly was concerned. Pauline started to read the letter out loud:

Dear Pauli,

I have great news! Mom is still alive after all these years. A kind lady that cares for her visited me at the diner. I know where she is, but I think we should go together. Can you come here? Try and get here as soon as possible. She said mom's not doing so well.

Love,

Josie

"That's great, Pauline, you have to go and visit her." Dolly was thrilled to hear her friend's good news.

Pauline choked up. She couldn't respond. Walter reached for her hand. "I'll take you to see her." Pauline smiled as she wiped away her tears.

"We are finishing up finals now. In a few days, I'll get my diploma. Can you take me then? I want her to see it. She'll be thrilled."

"Yes, it would be my pleasure."

WHAT'S OLD IS NEW AGAIN
1939

CHAPTER 23

A Dream Realized

Pauline couldn't wait for graduation day. It was a long, grueling journey for her and she wanted to savor every moment of it. Along with 149 other ladies, Pauline sat eagerly in her chair waiting for her name to be called. Dolly glanced back at Pauline who sat a few rows away. She wished they were sitting together. Sister Margaret relished in the day. She slowly and deliberately called out each student's name. The anticipation was too much for Pauline who kept fidgeting in her seat. Finally Sister Margaret said, "Pauline Roka." The sound of applause filled the room as Dolly screamed and Walter whistled. Grinning from ear to ear, Pauline walked to the front of the room to receive her diploma. She was ecstatic.

Sister Margaret knew that Pauline had beaten the odds and couldn't contain her happiness either. "You did it, Pauline. I'm so proud of you." Pauline accepted the diploma and was overcome with emotion. Uncharacteristically, she hugged the nun right in front of the crowd. Tears streamed down her cheeks as she glanced at Dolly who was crying too. She searched for Walter in the crowd. Spotting him in the back of the room, they locked eyes as he blew her a kiss. Walter proudly watched her take a seat. He couldn't wait to hug her.

After the ceremony, Pauline walked arm in arm with Dolly, laughing and smiling as they passed Millie. Pauline stopped and called out, "Congratulations, Millie. It's a great day for us all."

Caught off guard by Pauline's well wishes, Millie's face turned a pinkish red. "Yes it is, congratulations. You too, Dolly." Dolly nodded in return.

They continued to look for Walter. Leaning against the wall, holding a small bouquet of flowers, Walter smiled brightly when he saw them approach. He wrapped his arms around Pauline, twirling her around as he hugged her tightly. Her legs lifted off the ground and she felt like she was flying both figuratively and emotionally. Walter gave her a big kiss. "Congratulations. You did it!" He turned to Dolly and gave her a friendly hug. "And you too, Dolly, congratulations."

"I can't wait for tonight. What a party we'll have to celebrate!" Dolly exclaimed.

"Oh, Dolly, I'm not going to be there. We're going to meet my sister and visit my mother today." Pauline held up her diploma. "I can't wait to show her this. She's going to be so happy."

"How can I celebrate without you? I wish you were going to be here." Dolly saw the happiness drain from her friend's face. "But, I understand. I would do the same thing. We'll celebrate when you get back."

"I'll see you later. Thank you for being such a good friend. I couldn't have done this without you." Pauline sincerely meant it.

"Yes you could've!" Dolly hugged her. "Now go see your mother." Walter placed his arm around Pauline as they walked away. They savored this moment together and didn't say a word until they got into the car. She snuggled up close to him as he drove.

"I really appreciate you taking a day off to do this for me." She looked at his handsome face. He was so confident and strong all the time, but more importantly, he was always there for her.

Walter held her hand. "I'm just glad I can be a part of this with you. It truly means a lot to me."

Beaming with happiness, Pauline rattled on. "I can't wait until you meet my sister. You're going to love her."

"Are you sure she knows we're coming?" he asked.

"Of course."

"Tell me what she's like."

Pauline started to laugh. "She's the exact opposite of me in every way. It's hard to believe we're even sisters."

"You both care about and protect each other. That's the best kind of sister to have."

Pauline thought how right he was. The best kind.

Pauline was excited and nervous when they arrived in Lodi. She hadn't been back since she left a few years ago but everything looked exactly the same. She couldn't wait to see her sister again and had been fidgeting the whole trip. Almost sprinting down the street, Pauline suddenly stopped in front of the Lodi Orphanage. "What's the matter, Pauline?"

"That's the place, Walter. That's where I grew up," she said pointing at the two-story building.

Walter looked at her childhood home and really wanted to get closer. "Can we go in? I would love to meet the nun you always speak about."

Pauline hesitated. She was embarrassed by the condition of the orphanage which was in desperate need of repairs. Compared to the home where Walter was raised, it was in shambles. He grabbed her hand and gently pulled her through the gate. "Come on, let's go. We're right here."

Pauline still resisted. "It's been a long time since I left."

"Only a few years," he exclaimed. "Seriously, didn't the nun help you apply to nursing school? She would want to hear the good news too."

Pauline knew he was right, so she reluctantly agreed. Sister Sarah did so much for her. She would want to know.

As they walked up the front steps, he slowed his pace so she would be ahead of him. Pauline knocked while Walter stood slightly behind her waiting for the door to open. It seemed to take forever. Pauline was practically jumping out of her skin but it gave Walter a chance to look around and take it all in. He was enjoying the wait.

Finally, the door opened and Sister Sarah stood in the doorway. She was shocked to see Pauline. "Pauline, my dear child, what a pleasant surprise." She hugged her tight for a moment and then held her at arm's length to look her over. She was thrilled to see she was doing well. "What brings you back?"

"I did it. I finally graduated!" Pauline waved her diploma.

"I always knew you would. I never doubted you for one second. Won't you please come in and tell me about it. Who is this young man?"

"This is my friend Walter," she said while stepping into the foyer.

Once inside, Walter extended his hand to greet the nun. "It's such a pleasure to meet you. Pauline talks about you all the time." They entered the office and Pauline looked around remembering all the time she spent in that room as a child. Everything looked exactly the same as the day she left.

"She was always a special girl and different from the others."

"Yes, she is definitely unlike any other woman I've met before." Walter looked at her affectionately. Turning back toward the nun he said, "You did a fine job raising her."

"Pauline wasn't any trouble at all. She was always determined to make something out of herself from the start." Walter couldn't stop smiling. The nun reaffirmed everything he already thought about Pauline. "Have you seen Josephine yet? She's working across the street at the diner."

"No, not yet. We're picking her up and then visiting my mother. We now know where she's been all these years."

"I'm so happy for you two. Many young girls here never get that opportunity."

"It's all because of you. You've done so much for us." Pauline truly meant it.

"It's a blessing and God's will."

"I can't wait to see my mom, but I'm really nervous. I was eight years old when I last saw her and so much has changed," Pauline confessed to Sister Sarah. She was secretly hoping for some reassurance from her older confidant.

"Pauline, you have grown to be an exceptional young woman. Your mother is going to be so proud of you. You'll be fine."

Pauline and Sister Sarah hugged one last time. Walter noticed the true affection these two women shared for each other. "Pauline, be sure to come back and give me all the details. I'll be waiting for you."

"I will."

"It was truly a pleasure to meet you," Walter said to the nun. As they walked down the stairs together, Walter reached for Pauline's hand. She looked at him affectionately. He smiled, taking in her warmth and said, "Sister Sarah is wonderful. She's exactly as you described her. Thank you for letting me into this part of your life." They had taken a big step forward as a couple and he couldn't have been more pleased.

Crossing the street toward the diner, Pauline started to walk faster. Walter quickened his step to keep up with her. She was anxious to finally see her sister again. Walter opened the diner door to allow Pauline to enter. Standing there looking around, Pauline saw her sister racing toward her with a huge grin on her face. Josephine barreled into her almost knocking her over and they hugged for a long while. "I miss you so much, Pauli."

"Me too, Josie. Me too."

"Wow, is this him? He's very handsome."

"Hello, Josephine, it's a pleasure to meet you." Walter extended his hand for her to shake. Josephine disregarded his hand and threw her arms around him, hugging him as well. Walter started to laugh. He had never been greeted like that before.

Walter glanced toward Pauline. She smiled and shrugged. "That's Josie."

"What took you so long? I've been waiting."

"We stopped to see Sister Sarah before coming. I wanted to share my good news with her."

Thomas walked over and stood next to Josephine. She started introductions. "Thomas, this is my sister Pauline and her friend Walter. This is Thomas. He owns the diner."

Walter shook his hand while Pauline said, "Thank you so much for all you do for my sister. I know she really appreciates this and we're so grateful."

"She's the best waitress we have," Thomas said, "and the hardest worker."

"After all those years of scrubbing bathroom floors, this is a piece of cake." Josephine jokingly chimed in.

They all laughed as Walter thought to himself how nice it was to see Pauline happy and content.

Turning toward her sister, Josephine became very serious. "Pauli, I can't wait to see mom. How do I look?"

"You look great. Now, come on. Let's go see her before it gets too late."

The two girls talked nonstop during the car ride to the institution. Walter kept quiet, pleased that they were catching up after being apart for so long.

Once Walter pulled the car up to the front of the iron gate, he read the weathered sign, Woodlands, as Pauline reached for her diploma. "Oh, Josie, here it is. It's really true."

Josephine opened it up and screamed, "I can't believe it. My sister's a nurse. I'm so proud of you!"

Laughing at her outburst Walter elaborated, "She worked hard for this. She deserves it."

"Josie, I couldn't have done it without your help. Staying with Aunt Bertha was torture. I don't know how I'll ever repay you."

"Repay me? You're my sister. We protect each other. That's what sisters do."

"Yes, the best kind," Pauline said and reached for Walter's hand acknowledging his earlier statement. Walter flashed Pauline a warm smile, glad she remembered.

"Mom is going to be so proud. She always wanted you to continue your studies and become a nurse." Josephine innocently broke their moment.

"I'm going to show this diploma to her." Pauline attempted to fix her hair. At the thought of seeing her mother after all these years, she became jittery.

Walter noticed her restlessness and said, "Pauline, relax, you look beautiful."

Josephine teased. "She's the worrywart."

"I just want to look good for mom." Pauline shot back defending herself.

Pauline, Josephine, and Walter followed the guard's instructions and walked through the building entrance together. They approached the counter. Walter looked around, observing the hospital while the girls anxiously waited for the lady behind the counter to look up.

Finally she said, "May I help you?"

"We're here to see Ada Roka."

The lady reached in a drawer and pulled out a binder. With her index finger, she slid it down the list of names.

"I don't see her name here," the lady said as she slammed the binder closed.

"She's been here for a long time. Could you please check again?" Josephine asked politely.

After the same routine, the lady shook her ahead. "She's not on the list."

Josephine's voice rose. "She's got to be. She's our mother and we haven't seen her in thirteen years!" Softening her tone, she said, "Please, please can you check one more time?"

The lady saw her desperation. "Okay, let me check in the back."

Pauline glanced at her sister before addressing the lady. "Thank you for checking, it really means a lot to us."

The lady stood up and walked toward the back room. Restlessly, Pauline started fixing her hair again.

"Pauline, I told you already, you look beautiful." Walter reassured her.

Lena walked into the room ahead of the lady. She paused when she saw the three of them waiting. Josephine spotted her right away and said, "Pauli, that's the lady I was telling you about who cares for mom. I can't believe we're going to see her."

Lena deeply sighed before speaking. She didn't know what to say.

Pauline sensed something was wrong when she saw Lena's troubled look. She started fidgeting with her hair again.

Walter stepped closer to Pauline and tilted his head up, closing his eyes. As a doctor he had seen this look before and sensed the news wasn't good.

"Hello, Josephine." Lena smiled. "And is this Pauline?"

Josephine wasn't in the mood for small talk. "Yes. Can you please take us to see our mother now?"

Lena started to speak, but she was unable to get any words out. Trying to continue, she broke down into tears.

As always, Josephine looked to Pauline for answers. "Pauli, what's going on? Where's mom?" Pauline stood silently.

Once Lena composed herself, she started to explain. "I'm so sorry. I did my best. She knew you two were coming soon and tried to hang on."

Hearing the words spoken out loud, Lena felt their loss and hugged Pauline. Josephine joined them. All three cried while hugging each other. Overcome with sadness for Pauline and her sister, Walter watched from a distance and gave them space.

Lena broke away from the girls and reached into her pocket. She pulled out Ada's rosary beads. "She wanted to make sure that I gave you these. Your mom said you used to pray together."

Pauline nodded and started to well up with tears again. She took them from Lena and rubbed her fingers along the beads, the same way her mother always did. Walter put his arm around her. He couldn't take her pain away, but he could comfort her.

Watching Pauline stroke the beads, Lena was reminded of Ada. "She loved you two so much. She talked about you all the time and was so worried about you. Your mother never knew where you were until I found Josephine." Lena looked over at Josephine who was just standing there with tears streaming down her cheeks. "Once I told her you both were okay, she seemed at peace. Here's the locket with your pictures your mother stared at all the time." Handing it to Pauline Lena said, "She didn't have anything else."

Pauline asked for some more details. "Did anyone ever come visit her?"

"No." Lena shook her head.

"When did she pass?"

"Two days ago. I think you girls should know, your mom wanted your lives to be better than hers. She wanted more for you than just cooking and cleaning for a man."

"What do you mean?" Josephine asked.

Lena continued explaining. "I mean, she loved you both more than anything else in this world. She wanted you to be able to pursue your dreams, to study, to work, and to be able to choose your own future path." Lena looked down to think for a moment before continuing. "Your father had a different attitude about a woman's position and that's why he institutionalized her."

"Pauli, what is she saying?"

"Josie, she is saying that mom wanted us to have opportunities, like me going to nursing school. Dad didn't want that for us."

"That's exactly right," Lena said. "She was truly ahead of her time."

"Thank you for taking such good care of her. She was lucky to have you," Pauline said.

"Promise me that you won't let her journey die. Please make sure her story is always told."

Teary-eyed, Pauline glanced at Walter before looking at Lena. She said, "I promise."

The ladies hugged. Walter opened his arms wide and wrapped them around them all.

Once inside the car, it was eerily quiet. Gazing out the window, Josephine was heartbroken. Even after all these years of not seeing her mother, the finality of her passing really hurt. Pauline continued to rub the rosary beads she held tight. Walter looked over to check on the ladies often, but didn't say a word.

Pauline was the first to break the silence. "It's all my fault. I'm sorry, Josie."

"It's not your fault."

"I should have come right away, as soon as I got your letter. I just wanted to surprise mom with my diploma."

Seeing family members receive troubling news all the time, Walter chimed in. "You can't put this on yourself, Pauline. It's not fair. You had nothing to do with her death."

"We missed her by two days. I should have come the day I got the letter," she quickly snapped at Walter.

"Pauli, you had to finish your exams and graduate. It's not your fault. Walter's right. We're lucky that we even found out after all these years. She's happier in heaven than stuck in that hospital dad put her in."

"Still, I'll never forgive myself." Pauline started to silently pray the rosary. Walter glanced her way concerned.

Upon arriving at the diner Josephine said, "Why don't you two come in and eat something before your long drive back?"

"We really should get back on the road," Pauline said. "We both have to work tomorrow."

The two sisters embraced for a long time before letting go. Walter gave Josephine a hug. "I'm glad to finally meet you. I'm really sorry about today."

"It's okay. Thank you for driving us."

"Josie, why don't you take the night off?"

"I already said I'd work. It will keep me busy and my mind off of everything."

Pauline watched her little sister head toward the diner. She worried about her being alone. She wanted to stay with her.

"Do you still want to see Sister Sarah? She wanted us to go back." Pauline looked at Walter and nodded yes.

When they arrived at the orphanage, Sister Sarah was waiting for them and immediately greeted them at the front door with a huge smile. But, after she noticed Pauline's long face, she glanced at Walter who shook his head no. "Oh dear," the nun said.

"I waited too long. I should have come sooner," Pauline said to Sister Sarah as tears streamed down her face.

"Sometimes God has different plans for us. We never know what life will bring. Only He knows." Pauline bowed her head down. "Look at me." Picking up her head, Pauline looked at Sister Sarah with swollen, blood shot eyes. "Never think this is your fault. You must move on and not carry this burden. This was out of your control. You must follow your calling in life. That you can control." Sister Sarah squeezed her hands tightly and felt the rosary beads dangling from Pauline's hand. "Where did you get those?"

"The nurse gave them to me. They belonged to my mother."

"Always cherish them, my dear. Keep them close to your heart." Sister Sarah noticed Pauline rubbing her fingers over the beads. "Pauline, remember to always keep the determination and will that has been in you since you were a child. Life takes unexpected turns but always remember to follow your dreams."

Hugging Walter goodbye, Sister Sarah whispered into his ear, "Please take care of her. She needs you now."

"I will." Walking back toward the sidewalk, Walter put his arm around Pauline. He couldn't imagine what she was feeling but felt more love and admiration for her now than ever. He had to let her know. He stopped before the gate and turned her toward him and said, "You are the strongest woman I know. I am here for you always and want you to know how much I love you."

Pauline gazed into his loving eyes. "I love you too."

He pulled her closely to him as Pauline cried into his shoulder. Stroking her back, he held her tight. After a long while, he released his grip but held her close as they walked through the gate. Walter peeked at his wristwatch. "I know it's late and we have to work tomorrow, but we haven't eaten all day. Let's get something to eat before heading back. We have a long drive."

Pauline agreed.

CHAPTER 24

❧

I Promise

Meanwhile at the diner, Thomas watched Josephine wrap the apron around her waist. He had grown fond of her and knowing the challenges she faced in her short life already, he was hoping that she would finally receive some good news. As soon as Josephine glanced his way with swollen red eyes, his heart broke. Deflated, she walked over to him and said, "We missed her. She passed away two days ago."

"I'm so sorry, Josephine. Why don't you take the rest of the day off?"

"No, I want to work. Being busy will keep my mind off of it." Walking to the end of the counter to pick up her pad, she didn't notice her father walk in and slide into a booth.

Thomas immediately approached him suspecting Josephine wasn't in the mood to deal with him. "Not today, sir. Please leave."

"I just want a cup of coffee," Harry said gruffly.

"Not today, please come back another day." Thomas persisted.

"This is a free world, ain't it? Get me a cup of coffee."

Josephine heard her father's voice and quickly walked to the booth. She calmly said, "You can't keep coming here. This is where I work."

"You don't look too good today. What's the matter?"

"Nothing, please leave. I don't want to see you anymore." Josephine fought back tears. She didn't want to cry in front of her father.

"I need help. I'm sick." Harry coughed gasping for air.

"Then, go see a doctor."

"I don't have money for a doctor."

"Maybe you shouldn't spend all your money on booze then."

"I lost my job. I have no more money."

The front door opened. Pauline walked in and was shocked to see her sister talking to their father. Annoyed and hoping to get rid of him once and for all, Josephine reached into her apron pocket and pulled out some change. She tossed coins on the table. "Now, go see a doctor and get out! Don't ever come back here again."

Startled by what she saw, Pauline hurried to the table. "Josie, why are you giving money to dad?"

Surprised to see Pauline standing there, Harry provoked his oldest daughter. "Ah, the older sister comes to her protection. Just like she did with her mother." Harry glanced back toward Thomas. "I'm still waiting for my coffee. Where is it?"

Thomas quickly arrived with a cup of coffee spilling half of it as he rushed across the floor. Walter was now by the girls' side.

Pauline turned to Josephine and demanded an answer, "Josie, what are you doing?" Josephine stood silent, unsure how to respond.

"She's helping her father out. That's what she's doing." Harry smirked as he took a sip of coffee. Gasping for air he said, "That's right. She's always been the one with heart."

Stunned, Walter whispered to Pauline, "Is this your father?"

Pauline nodded as she reached across the table and swiped the change. Glaring at her father she screamed, "You have no right taking money from her."

Harry's temper was rising. He stood up and said, "Why don't you and your pretty boyfriend take a walk to wherever you came from. But first, give me my money."

"You're being very rude, sir. Apologize to your daughter." Walter couldn't keep quiet any longer.

Harry leaned in closely to Walter's face. "Do you have a problem with me?" Seeing this often when she was a child, Pauline didn't hesitate to step in between Walter and her father. Harry pushed her away and she went crashing onto the floor. Walter bent down to help her up, while keeping one eye on Harry.

"Ah, what a nice boy you got here. He's even helping you up. Now give me the money you stole from me."

Thomas saw the other customers watching the commotion. "This has to stop! Please, this is a place of business."

Josephine looked at her sister and said, "Pauli, just give him the money so he will leave, please."

Suddenly, Harry started to violently cough. He tumbled over, barely able to stand up, and collapsed to the floor.

Walter immediately bent down. "Sir, sir, can you hear me?" Noticing he was pale and unresponsive, he felt for a pulse and quickly started pressing on his chest. "Someone call for an ambulance." Thomas scurried away.

Pauline and Josephine stood still and watched Walter attempt to save their father's life. Neither one could believe this was happening, especially after just finding out their mother's heartbreaking news.

Walter glanced up toward Pauline. "I need your help. Come here." While her father was unconscious on the floor, Pauline heard Walter but didn't have the heart to help him.

Seeing her hesitation Walter said, "This is the time you need to put your personal feelings aside." Walter tried to talk some sense into her as he pressed on Harry's chest.

"But, you don't understand—"

He cut her off mid-sentence. "What I do understand is you recently took a pledge. Father or not, you are a nurse first and he's a person in need. Now, please come here."

Reluctantly, Pauline bent down and assisted Walter until an ambulance arrived. Once the medics raced in, Walter updated them on Harry's condition. He was responsive but still groggy and dazed. It appeared that Walter saved Harry's life, but Pauline didn't care. Her concern now was for Josephine and what would become of her with their father's return. Pauline approached Josephine who was talking to Thomas.

"I'm sorry about the mess today."

"It's not your fault."

"Yes it is. He came here because of me and disrupted everything."

Feeling the responsibility of being the older sister, Pauline interjected, "That's right. That's why you're coming back to New York with me."

"But this is all I know."

Pauline glanced at her father as the medics began to roll him on a stretcher. Seeming more alert, Harry locked eyes with Pauline and unleashed a devilish grin. Pauline's blood started to boil and she didn't respond to her sister. As the medics passed by with the stretcher, Pauline firmly grabbed hold of the end causing it to come to an abrupt stop.

Glaring at Harry, Pauline leaned right up to his face and said, "We never want to see you again. Just stay out of our lives like you always have." Walter heard Pauline's echoing voice and rushed to her side. Grabbing hold of her, he tried to coax her to remove her tight grip from the stretcher.

"Pauline, let them go."

Not that she wished for her father to die, but all the pent up anger from the day showed on her flushed face. She wanted to make sure he knew her plan. "I'm taking Josephine away. I'll make sure you never bother her again."

Harry's pale face became flushed again. "You both owe me your lives. If I didn't do what I –"

"We owe you nothing. Just leave us alone," Pauline snapped back without hesitation.

"You can't hide forever from me. I'll find you one day."

Pauline released her grip as the medics wheeled him away. Harry smirked at Pauline right before the stretcher was rolled out the front door. Impatiently, Pauline glanced toward Josephine. "It's not safe here anymore for you. He'll be back to haunt you."

"But, Pauli, he's sick and won't be back."

"Trust me, he will, just to cause problems. Look what he has done to our family already."

Pauline turned toward Thomas. "I'm really sorry, sir, but Josie is coming back with me to New York."

Although Thomas didn't want to lose Josephine as a worker, he knew what Pauline said was true after what he had just witnessed. "I hate to lose her. She's a great worker and all the customers love her."

"I know you've been watching out for her, but he'll never let it go. As you've just seen, he's not a good man."

Thomas nodded in agreement. Over the past few days, he had witnessed how manipulative and abusive Harry could be. He admired Josephine and hoped for her safety.

"Let's go, Josie."

Sadly, Josephine gave Thomas a big hug. "Thank you for everything you've done for me. I'll be forever grateful to you."

"You haven't been here for long, but I will miss you dearly."

"I'll clear my room out and give you this month's rent."

"Don't worry about the rent, just worry about yourself right now." Josephine hugged Thomas one last time and then walked to the door. "Josephine!" She turned back to face Thomas. "You're welcome back here anytime."

After all that has happened, the kindness from this gentleman brought a grin to her sad face.

After Josephine packed her belongings, she slid into the backseat of the car. Walter began the long journey back to New York. Everyone was exhausted. Their eyes were heavy and bloodshot. It was an emotional day filled with highs and lows. Walter reached out to hold Pauline's hand. She yanked it away and stared out the window. Surprised, Walter glanced her way. "Pauline, what's wrong?"

"I can't believe you made me help him," she snapped.

"This is the occupation we both chose. There will be plenty of rotten people that you won't want to help but will have to."

"Still, it wasn't right. You have no idea what he has put us through, and as you just witnessed, still putting us through." Overcome by the day's events, Pauline welled up again with tears. She turned to glance out the window.

"Even though he's a bad man and a terrible father, in time you'll know what I mean. You're now a nurse first before anything else."

"Pauli, he's right. You had no choice but to help."

Pauline lashed out at her sister, "And when did you plan on telling me he was around?"

"I was going to tell you soon. I just didn't want it to ruin your graduation and trip to see mom."

"This was news I should have known. We have never kept secrets from one another."

"I wanted today to be special for you. That's it."

Pauline stared out the window and kept her thoughts to herself. She couldn't believe all that had happened in one day. Her mother's encouragement had given her the confidence to believe in herself and she had received her diploma after years of struggling and hard work. She knew her mother was now in heaven watching over her. After all they had been through, Pauline held her diploma tightly, comforted by the knowledge that their shared dream had finally come true.

Pauline reached into her pocket and pulled out her mother's rosary beads. She rubbed them between her fingers and soaked in the comfort they brought her. She knew her mother was with her today.

Gazing out the back window, Josephine was furious with her father for uprooting her life again. She couldn't believe that this was happening to her. Trying to make sense of where she was heading, Josephine broke the silence. "Pauli, where am I going to live now?"

"I'm not sure yet."

"But I know nothing about New York."

Walter took this opportunity to help ease their minds. "When I volunteered at the Mt. Vernon Infirmary, there was a nice, Italian lady that I cared for. She owns a big house and rents out rooms. We can see if she has anything available if you want?"

"I guess that sounds okay. What do you think, Pauli?"

"How far is it from me? I want to make sure she's close by."

"It's the next town over. I think there's even a train or bus that goes back and forth."

Josephine perked up. "Oh wow, that would be great."

"We'll have to see what it costs first, Josie. You're not working right now."

Walter said, "I think she owns a small diner in town too. With Josephine's experience, I'm sure she'll be glad to offer her a job." Walter glanced at Josephine. "You'll love her. She's bubbly like you."

Josephine was excited. "I can't wait to meet her!"

"Okay, we'll go see her soon."

Walter continued driving in silence as everyone turned to their own thoughts again. His mind started racing thinking about all that Pauline had gone through and still continued to endure. He now understood that they were from totally different worlds like his mother had said.

As Pauline's thoughts drifted she blurted out, "She is right, you know?"

"Who?" Josephine didn't have a clue who her sister was talking about.

"Lena, the lady that took care of mom. We have to make sure mom's story is always told. We can't let it just end like this."

Walter chose his words carefully to not upset Pauline any further. "I agree. I never met your mother, but I can see where your strength and determination comes from. I'm sure she was a fascinating lady."

"She was." Pauline rubbed the rosary beads. "We have to continue on, Josie, in memory of mom. We can't let this end our journey or hers. She would want that from us."

"I know she would. We came this far already."

"Yes, and we'll continue on our path with the memory of mom by our side. Always."

As they traveled over the George Washington Bridge, they caught a glimpse of the sunset. It was a spectacular view and their minds slowly drifted with ease to their own thoughts. The yellow and orange hues were peaceful and soothing. As they admired the sunset over the beautiful New York City skyline, they were forever determined to make sure that the next chapter in their journey would continue to make their mother proud.